"I KNOW WHAT I WANT." AND WHAT HE WANTED was her lips. Right now. He could see nothing beyond them, and she knew it.

"No, Jack," she said breathlessly. "I don't think you ought to do what you're thinking of doing."

"I'm through thinking about it, Kary. And this time I'm going to do it right."

Part of her eagerly, shamelessly craved the kiss, but the rational side of her told her to run.

"Look at me, Kary."

She hadn't realized she'd closed her eyes, but when she opened them and gazed into the dark blue depths of his, she saw unmistakable desire there, and it fed her own. This was what she'd been wanting for days, what she'd been wanting for so much longer than that. "Jack . . ." she whispered.

"Yes." His hands framed her face, thumbs stroking the corners of her mouth, and then the magic began. . . .

WHAT ARE *LOVESWEPT* ROMANCES?

They are stories of true romance and touching emotion. We believe those two very important ingredients are constants in our highly sensual and very believable stories in the LOVESWEPT line. Our goal is to give you, the reader, stories of consistently high quality that may sometimes make you laugh, sometimes make you cry, but are always fresh and creative and contain many delightful surprises within their pages.

Most romance fans read an enormous number of books. Those they truly love, they keep. Others may be traded with friends and soon forgotten. We hope that each LOVESWEPT romance will be a treasure—a "keeper." We will always try to publish

LOVE STORIES YOU'LL NEVER FORGET
BY AUTHORS YOU'LL ALWAYS REMEMBER

The Editors

SECRET ADMIRER

LINDA JENKINS

BANTAM BOOKS

NEW YORK · TORONTO · LONDON · SYDNEY · AUCKLAND

SECRET ADMIRER
A Bantam Book / September 1993

If you would be interested in receiving protective vinyl covers for your
Loveswept books, please write to this address for information:

Loveswept
Bantam Books
P.O. Box 985
Hicksville, NY 11802

ISBN 0-553-44313-5

Published simultaneously in the United States and Canada

PRINTED IN THE UNITED STATES OF AMERICA

OPM   0 9 8 7 6 5 4 3 2 1

ONE

Halfway through the backdoor, Karolyn Lucas stumbled over a pair of large, dirty sneakers. She froze. All her senses went on instant alert. A strange tickling sensation settled in her stomach. She swallowed. It tasted metallic. Her heartbeat raced from a surge of adrenaline.

Someone had ransacked the house!

Five days before, when she'd left for the molecular-science symposium in Iowa City, everything had been in order. Now the kitchen counters were cluttered with boxes, bags, and cans of food. Piles of clothing were strewn over the small round breakfast table and its four chairs.

Quietly, carefully, she set down her suitcase to prop open the screen. The unwelcome rush of Galveston's muggy ninety-five-degree August air was a small price to pay in case she needed an escape route.

On tiptoe she crept toward the dining room, snagging one of her mother's antique rug beaters from a collection decorating the yellow wall. For added protection, she lifted a heavy, old-fashioned iron off the pie safe.

The swinging door creaked when she eased it open with one shoulder. Karolyn cringed, then stood still, listening. Not a sound except the distant, rhythmic click of Mrs. Potter's hedge trimmers.

She stole past the George III breakfront, where the late-afternoon sun reflected in the silver on its shelves. She frowned. Didn't burglars usually snitch the sterling before trashing closets and kitchen cabinets?

Flattening herself against the wall, she peeked around the facing of an open double doorway that led into the living room. Nothing out of place in there. Tightening her grip, she continued her silent advance.

A muffled snore, then a deep sigh drifted up from the sofa. At the same time a large, bare foot draped itself over the scrolled arm. A sleeping burglar couldn't pose much of a threat, so she raised her weapons and edged close enough to peer over the back of the settee.

Her breath caught. She blinked rapidly. The rest of him was nearly as bare as his foot, the vivid purple shorts a meager concession to modesty. She hadn't seen him for twelve years, but those years had treated him kindly. There was no mistaking her visitor. He was brawnier, more manly, and a hundred times better looking in the flesh than in any of her fanciful imaginings.

Recognition spurred her heart to beat even faster. Her legs threatened to buckle. The ten-pound iron slid from her grasp and narrowly missed crushing her big toe as it thudded onto the thick Chinese rug. "You," she breathed.

One eye slitted open. He was the only person she'd ever known with eyes so dark a blue they could pass for navy. "Hey, Kary. How's my favorite brainiac?" His other eye opened and he studied her, a sly smile parting lips that were indecently sensual on a man. "Discovered any interesting germs lately? Or have you traded in your trusty microscope for something bigger and better?"

Admiration transformed to fury in a nanosecond. Jack Rowland's teasing had always been a part of her life. This time she vowed he wouldn't get the best of her. "Some things never change. You're still the same smart-ass you always were."

"And you're still quick to rise to the bait."

Glaring, she swung the rug beater back and forth aggressively. "Careful, my hand might slip."

"What are you waving that thing around for, anyway? Planning to whip me into shape, like your mother threatened a time or two?"

She glanced from him to her weapon and back before lowering it. "The idea has a certain appeal." He flashed his trademark bad-boy grin. No doubt it would have disarmed someone who didn't know him quite so well. Karolyn recognized it for what it was—a harbinger of mischief. "Don't push your luck. I thought you were a burglar, so I armed myself with the first thing available."

He rolled his eyes. "Kary, if you've walked in on a burglar, you should turn right back around, go straight to a neighbor's, and call the police. Surely you know that much."

She did know it . . . intellectually. But she'd charged ahead without thinking, impulsive instead of rational. Such unpredictable behavior was getting to be a habit, an increasingly disturbing pattern. At the moment, however, she had an even more disturbing problem on her hands. "Spare me the lecture. I'm well aware of proper safety procedures."

"Yep, same old IQ Lucas. Smarter than anybody within five states, and not afraid to show it."

She drew in a sharp breath, swamped by old memories. For as long as she could recall, she'd endured jokes about her intelligence. For just as long, she had tried to ignore them, rarely succeeding. In her mind, being brainy equated with being different, an outsider. But she'd sooner sit in a bed of fire ants than let anyone, especially this man, see that he'd scored a hit where she was most vulnerable. "What are you doing in my house, Jack Rowland?"

"Sleeping off a monster case of jet lag." He yawned and stretched, a lazy extension of his lithe, tanned body that set off a restless stirring inside her. Then he came up on one elbow, threw back his head, yawned again, and rubbed his chest.

Karolyn swallowed, pretending sudden absorption in a pair of framed watercolors over the slate mantel. The pictures didn't dispel the image of exposed skin and well-honed muscles. The man had a body that would distract any woman with breath left in her. "I suppose your jet lag is an occupational hazard. The question is, why are you using my living-room couch to sleep it off?"

"I have a standing invitation from your brother."

That traitor! He'd never mentioned a word to

her about any sort of invitation. She studied Jack for a sign that he was pulling her leg. In the past, a funny little quirk of his lips had always given him away. She saw no hint of it today. "Clint's not here."

"I know. We crossed paths earlier this week in Singapore." He consulted his watch, a bulky black gizmo that spanned his right wrist. "By now he's offshore, in the Gulf of Malaysia. Probably be gone at least a month."

He sounded overly pleased by her brother's absence, which made her wary. "Then I can't imagine why you chose this particular time to visit Galveston."

He unfolded slowly and rose to face her, his expression solemn. "All at once it hit me that I'd stayed away too long. I had this compelling urge to come home."

Karolyn had a compelling urge to put a Texas mile between them. Jack wasn't unusually tall—not much over six feet—and she was no shrimp at five-seven. But he'd always been a male who emitted enough magnetism to rival the super collider.

Perversely fascinated, she had watched a continual parade of witless teenage girls succumb, wondering how they could act so silly over such an obvious pest. Through it all, she'd remained immune to his charms. Or so she'd repeatedly told herself. Today she was getting an up-close and personal taste of what the fuss was all about. "How can you call this home? You haven't been back since high-school graduation."

"My parents may have moved sixteen years ago, but I grew up here." He gestured west, toward where his family had lived, several blocks away. "I've always considered Galveston home. It makes sense that I'd eventually return."

"I imagine your nostalgia will be short-lived. This island will seem awfully tame compared to the exotic places you've stopped off since you left." She deliberately avoided any allusion to the scores of wild adventures he and her brother had shared during that time.

Drat! Now he'd make a big deal about her keeping track of him. And she *hadn't*, at least not by design. It was Clint's fault. There was more than one kind of pipeline in the oil business, and no matter where they were, the two men had managed to stay in contact.

He didn't make the sardonic comment she'd dreaded. Instead his steady gaze pinned her, making it difficult to breathe. "Exotic can be anywhere you're not, Kary. And lately Galveston has started looking like the most welcoming place on earth to me."

It won't last long, she warned herself in an

attempt to quell the curious excitement sparked by his declaration. Jack was a nomad, a thrill seeker, a womanizer. Definitely out of her league. "I give you two weeks at the most before someplace else starts to look better."

"Is that a bet?" Brows arched, he sauntered past her on his way to the staircase in the entry hall. "'Cause if it is, you're on."

Karolyn never bet on anything. Odds against winning were too great. "According to the law of statistical probabilities—" The doorbell chimed, cutting off her discourse. Jack was closer, so he answered it.

"For Ms. Lucas," a young male voice said.

She whirled around to watch Jack accept delivery of a modest bouquet. He set it down on the marble-top Duncan Phyfe table and poked through the foliage, searching in vain for a card. "Guess you'll have to call and find out who they're from."

A call would not be necessary. As she'd been checking out of her hotel this morning, she had spied a gorgeous arrangement on the counter, being held for the arrival of a female guest. Feeling sorry for herself because nobody ever sent her flowers *anywhere*, and because she was going back to an empty house and an empty weekend, she located a phone booth and ordered the bouquet as a welcome-home treat.

"Oh," she heard herself say blithely, "it's my secret admirer again. He's always surprising me like this." The bald-faced lie flew off her tongue so readily, she might have been rehearsing it for days.

"Hmmph!" His nose wrinkled, as if the saffron lilies, red carnations, yellow snapdragons, and assorted greenery smelled bad. "Any secret admirer worthy of the name ought to be more imaginative than this."

Her fingers clenched around the beater handle. He was so unbearably cocky, it would serve him right if she did swat him. His ridicule practically demanded that she defend the nonexistent suitor she'd created. "I suppose a resourceful man with your vast experience could do better?"

He leaned against the curly-pine newel post and crossed his arms. "There's not a doubt in my mind." Sunlight filtering through the yellow stained-glass window gilded the walnut-brown hair on his head and chest. He was once again the handsome golden prince of her youthful fantasies. "I can beat that guy at his own game, Kary, any day of the week. With one hand tied behind my back."

Scowling, Jack watched her scoop up the arrangement and sail off to the kitchen. She probably wanted to escape before he started asking questions. Wise move. That's exactly what he'd have done. Grilled her. He had a hunch the secret-admirer bit was a smoke screen; the breathless way Kary had explained it rang false. But they had come from someone, and the guy evidently sent them regularly enough that he didn't bother with a card.

"Damn!" He punched his palm with one fist. The realization that he had competition tightened Jack's gut. Why hadn't Clint told him? Of course, he hadn't leveled with Kary's brother about *all* the reasons for his return to Galveston. In spite of his grousing about her headstrong, opinionated ways, Clint maintained a protective eye on his sister. He most likely would have given Jack some static had he known his best friend was out to seduce and claim Kary.

Put that way it did sound a little primitive. But that was exactly why he'd come back.

He pushed away from the railing, ambled into the living room, and reclaimed his spot on the couch. As he lay staring at the twelve-foot ceiling, he replayed the long, circuitous journey that had led him back to his birthplace.

After too many years of bumming around, knowing too many women too casually, he finally understood why none of them meant as much as they should. He had always used the wrong criteria to pick them. If they looked great, liked to have fun, and didn't demand a lot of him, that was all he required. Then one morning almost a year ago he woke up and, in a sudden flash of insight, knew he'd had enough. In the months since, he'd never wavered, never strayed.

He was thirty-four and had raised more than his share of hell in places he'd forgotten. Now he was ready to settle down. To Jack, that meant a home, a wife, kids . . . and Galveston. For the rest of his life. He could accomplish it all so easily, except maybe the wife.

Once he'd begun to analyze what he really valued in a mate, the wife part had been easy too. Beauty was superfluous; so was the body. He wanted a woman he could talk to at breakfast as well as late at night. He wanted somebody with intelligence, who could think for herself, and tell him when he wasn't thinking clearly. He wanted . . . Kary.

She was the smartest person Jack had ever known, and his definition had nothing to do with test scores. When he had been sixteen, confident on the surface, but inside a mass of raging contradictions as to whether he was boy or man—and with a big decision facing him—Kary with her ten-year-old wisdom had helped make up his mind.

Late one steamy August night on the Lucases' front porch, she had said, "There are always plenty of people who act like they understand what you need." With her middle finger, she'd pushed up her thick glasses and aimed them at him. "Nobody *knows* what's best for you better than you do. Always remember that, Jack, and don't let someone else decide."

"Thanks, Kary," he now said softly. "You saved me then. Let's hope you're as generous now."

He understood that he couldn't just breeze back into town, announce his intentions, and expect to get his way. But he'd never run from a fight. If he had to battle another man for her affection, she was well worth the price. When the stakes were this high, he'd stop at nothing.

A short time later he joined her in the kitchen, confident that he was on the right track. "Uh-oh," he said when he saw that she'd dragged in a big box and dumped all his clothes into it. "Sorry about the mess."

"You and Clint are two of a kind, hauling dirty laundry from halfway around the globe. I think he clings to the eternal hope that someday I'll wash and iron it for him."

Jack began a mental list. *Number one, don't expect her to do the laundry.* "Here, let me get that out of your way." He bent to hoist the box and trotted out to the rear alley where he stashed it in the trunk of his rental car. Tomorrow was soon enough to figure out how he was going to get the bulk of his wardrobe clean.

Then he hurried back and found her pawing through the chaos he'd left on the counters. "Driving in on Sixty-First, I stopped by the Randalls' to pick up some bread and milk, cereal and eggs."

She balanced a can of litchi nuts in one hand and Bavarian sauerkraut in the other. One long-ago night in Spain, he'd gotten plastered drinking amontillado. Without the glasses, Kary's eyes were the same warm, seductive brown as that potent, unforgettable sherry. "It appears you took a detour down the wrong aisle."

"I hadn't shopped in a real supermarket in years and I sort of lost control. Just kept grabbing stuff and tossing it into the cart." He shrugged. "Ended up spending a hundred thirty-nine bucks."

"Well, it should be interesting to see what you

do with all this 'stuff.' You've the makings for several unusual meals, that's for sure."

Second on the list, she thinks you can cook. "Mmm," he agreed, wondering if he stood a chance of faking even basic kitchen skills. Why not? How hard could it be? Still, he wasn't all that eager to volunteer for KP yet. "Let's leave the groceries for now. How'd you like to eat out tonight?"

She walked over and picked up her suitcase. "I've spent the past few days in Iowa, where beef takes up most of the menu. I'd rather change, bike to Hill's, and get some fish or seafood to fix here."

"Hill's at the pier, you mean?" She nodded and he went on, "Why don't you go ahead and change. I'll run down there and pick up the fish. We can cook together."

When he saw her wavering, he didn't give her a chance to protest. "I'll be back in a few minutes." He dashed out the door, bypassing his shoes on the way.

Before he got in the car, he dug around in the box he'd stowed in the trunk, finally locating an old pair of running shoes and a T-shirt that was only semigrungy. Kary had kept staring at his bare chest, probably because she didn't approve. So be it. If she had a no-shirt, no-shoes, no-service policy, he'd do his best to comply. He aimed to please. "Your wish is my command." Jack chuckled. "Within reason, of course."

He drove to Water Street in record time by taking the back way. He had arrived just a couple of days ago, but one of the first things he'd noticed was that traffic had gotten a lot heavier during the years he'd been away. There was a steady stream of cars on Seawall and the Strand, and this evening's invasion of weekend tourists made both more congested than usual.

All the changes didn't bother him; he was too glad to be here to lament the past. He'd told Kary the truth about having always considered this his home. But only recently had he begun to appreciate how much he'd left behind.

The minute he had crossed the bridge over Galveston Bay, a sense of rightness had clicked into place deep inside him. He was happier, more stable, more optimistic than he'd been in ages, thanks to the woman waiting for him in the Silk Stocking Historic District house. He made the return trip in even less time.

Through the flow-glass pane of the backdoor, Jack could see Kary standing at the sink. She had replaced her full print skirt and matching blouse with pink shorts and a white low-necked top that exposed a narrow strip of skin when she bent or reached. His palms tingled.

At twelve she'd been a gangly, klutzy kid with her head continually crammed in a book, tripping over her own feet and legs every other step. The last time he'd seen her, at his and Clint's college graduation, she'd been sixteen and showing signs of promise, though he hadn't been discriminating enough then to appreciate them. Now she was twenty-eight and, man, had she ever caught up with those legs. Sweat beaded his forehead and gathered along his spine. He closed his eyes for a second and blew out a low whistle.

It was going to take a superhuman show of willpower not to rush this part of things. Once he'd decided what he wanted, he started wanting it all today. Unfortunately he also had to convince Kary that she wanted the same future.

Instinct told him the lady wouldn't be an easy sell. Because in addition to a future, they also shared a past. Jack didn't kid himself that she looked back on it—or him—with great fondness.

He added numbers three and four to his list. *Resist the urge to tease her, and whatever you do, keep your hands to yourself until she's ready*. At this rate the damned list was going to be so long he'd never be able to stay on top of everything.

Inserting the key Clint had supplied, he

pushed open the door. "Red snapper," he said when she turned. Like a Stone Age hunter with fresh kill, he offered it to his woman. The savage imagery startled him, sparked other urges that were even more primal.

"Oh, good." She accepted the package, unwrapped it, and sniffed the fish. He'd seen her mother do the same thing a hundred times. "We can cook this on the grill and save heating up the house."

"Sounds fine." The last thing he needed was more heat. If the past hour was any indication, the rest of the summer was going to be long and hot. "What can I do?"

"Build the fire. Charcoal and lighter are in the garage." She rolled out a drawer and produced a box of matches. "While it's burning down I'll make a salad and get the fish and corn ready for the coals."

Following orders, Jack trooped back outside to the garage in search of charcoal. "Look at me," he muttered, upending the bag to empty half its contents into a Weber kettle. "Turning into a regular Mr. Middle America."

He saturated the briquets, then struck a match. Flames erupted with a *whoosh* and shot skyward. He leaped back just in time to spare his eyebrows from getting singed. Must have overdone the lighter fluid. He slapped on the lid to cap the fire and was immediately engulfed in a cloud of smoke. This cooking business ought to qualify him for hazardous-duty pay.

"Everything under control?" Kary asked, sticking her head out the door.

He whisked off the lid, relieved to see that it had extinguished the blaze. "Everything's great." He blessed her timing. A few seconds earlier and she'd have witnessed his rendition of the inferno. "Should be ready in ten minutes or so." Did that sound about right?

Figuring he might be able to pick up a few pointers, either by observation or osmosis, he headed back inside to see what Kary was doing in the kitchen. She had three kinds of lettuce draining in a colander and was slicing and dicing her way through a mound of vegetables.

He found something cozy and satisfying in watching her do so mundane a chore as stripping carrots. Not that he'd ever tell her so. She'd probably turn on him with that deadly-efficient German peeler.

Jack braced his hips against the counter and casually inquired, "What's life like these days for Dr. Karolyn Lucas, genius-in-residence?"

The peeler went skittering into the sink. A slight flush spread over her chest and up her neck.

"Nothing you'd find very exciting, I'm sure." She switched to a wicked-looking knife and whacked the top off a tomato. "Why do you want to know?"

Suspicious already, and he'd only begun. "Just trying to catch up. Isn't that what old friends do when they haven't seen each other for a long time?"

"I guess. Is that how you see us, as old friends?"

"Absolutely. Come on, give. How do you spend your days?" His gaze lingered on her eyes, her mouth. "And nights."

She launched an attack on a bell pepper. "Work keeps me very busy. I'm currently studying polymerases and other enzymes in DNA, growth factors that can speed and effect cell replication. This area shows promise in the promotion of wound healing, but it has applications to all aspects of medicine, from heart attacks and strokes to burns and surgery. Anything involving tissue injuries that need repair."

He hadn't a clue. "A cure for cancer, maybe?"

She snapped to attention, brown eyes blazing. "If your intention is to make fun of me again, just pack up your groceries and your dirty clothes and go back where you came from. I'm not playing the little-sister role anymore, and I don't have to put up with you *or* your taunts."

"Hey, hey, take it easy," he soothed, touching her arm. Her skin was seductively soft. He wanted to stroke it, sate himself with it. Instead she had him on the defensive. "Where'd you get the idea that I would make fun of you?"

She flinched and said in a tight voice, "From past experience, naturally. You were the grand champion at putting me down." Half a dozen plump mushrooms fell victim to her slashing blade.

"Put you *down*?" Jack shook his head, incredulous. "I did no such thing." He had teased her some, sure, but mainly to get a reaction. She always cooperated. Kary had been such a feisty brat, annoyingly smart and lippy, quick with a comeback. To him, the baiting had represented a stimulating, harmless game they played with each other.

Apparently she had viewed it from a different perspective. Her accusation sounded resentful, almost bitter. Which put a different spin on his argument. "I swear, I never aimed to hurt you."

"Ha!" She tossed her head so defiantly her near-black braid flipped over one shoulder. "I'm sure you gave nary a thought to whether I'd be hurt or not. I was just a dumb, clumsy child to you then. Fair game. But let me tell you something, Jack Rowland, those days are long gone. I do not exist for your amusement." She punctuated each word with a jab of the knife.

"Uh, could you lay down that machete a second? I have the feeling I'm dangerously close to ending up pulverized like those vegetables."

As his words sank in she glowered at the mess she'd made. "Oh, poop," she mumbled disgustedly. "I let you get to me again." With exaggerated care she placed the knife on the cutting board, its sharp edge angled away from him. "I was right earlier. Some things never change."

Jack summoned his most earnest expression and directed the full force of it at her. "Wrong, Kary. You'll soon find out that I've changed a lot."

She made a prolonged ritual of washing and drying her hands. "I doubt if we'll be spending enough time together during your visit for me to see the new you."

Jack gritted his teeth. She thought he was just passing through. Before he could set her straight, she handed him the platter of thick snapper filets and corn wrapped in foil. "What do you think, five minutes to a side?"

"That ought to do it," he said, as if he were a renowned authority on grilling. Their conversation had raised his frustration level because it had veered off course. But at least she'd given him a tip that ensured he wouldn't screw up his assignment. He had planned on cooking the fish for an hour. The results of that experiment could have shingled a roof.

At the end of his alloted time, he transferred the finished product onto the platter and presented it for her approval. "Smells terrific. Looks perfect."

"Piece of cake," he said confidently, making a note to serve fish often. Cooking had turned out to be pretty simple after all. Some woman, somewhere, had once told him that no female could resist a man who cooked for her.

They served themselves from the counter and sat facing each other at the small table in the kitchen. Kary fussed with her silverware and repositioned her plate, as if his presence made her ill at ease. Surely not. He had been a regular fixture at the Lucas dining table. Picking up his fork, he dug in. After a few seconds she did the same. "I almost suggested eating on the deck. Ten minutes around that fire and I changed my mind. It's a sweatbox out there."

"You must have forgotten how hot it is in August."

"I've done time in several places more miserable than this." Jack swore silently. Best to steer clear of that phase in his life. He wanted to impress her as being something more than a vagabond engineer who'd take a contract anywhere in the world, as long as the price was high enough.

"Yes, Clint's told me about some of the . . . hot spots you've landed in."

Thanks a whole bunch, old buddy. You're really helping my cause. "Yeah, well, that's all behind me. I've turned over a new leaf."

She nodded, but didn't look the least bit convinced. "Now that I'm back, where will you go?"

He almost choked on a bite of romaine. So she was going to try to evict him. No way. "I had planned on staying here for a while."

She picked at the corner of her place mat. "Since Clint isn't due in for weeks, you'd probably be more comfortable elsewhere."

"I spent lots of time in this house. I'm perfectly comfortable here. It was like a second home to me for a long time, remember?"

"I remember." Did she have any idea how appealing she looked in full blush? "But under the circumstances . . ."

"What circumstances?" He watched her turn the snapper into mush. "Are you worried that we're here alone with nobody to chaperon?" He weighed his next question carefully. "Afraid I'll lose control and compromise you?"

She jerked upright, vibrating with indignation. "Of course not! I've never heard anything so ridiculous!" Then she wilted a little. "I'm not your type."

He wanted to contradict her, but took a different tack. "If that's the case, is there any reason we can't share the house . . . like you and Clint do?"

She chewed on her lip. He could see her formidable brain compiling evidence against him, so he played his trump card. "Come on. I'm practically one of the family. If your parents found out, they would insist that I live here."

"I know," she said with a resigned sigh. "Just tell me one thing. Approximately how long do you plan on staying?"

"Get used to cohabiting, Kary. I'm back in Galveston for good."

TWO

"What are we going to do today?"

Karolyn started at the sound of Jack's voice. His husky morning drawl unsettled her. The insinuation that they would be doing something together unsettled her. An intense awareness that he'd slept in the adjoining room last night unsettled her. To be honest, everything about the man unsettled her. Which was just infuriating. It was a point of honor that she not fawn over him like every other woman he'd ever met.

She framed her glass of orange juice with both hands, concentrating on the pulpy surface as hard as Madame Zora did on the tea leaves she read. For the hundredth time she told herself to forget Zora's prediction that a handsome stranger would enter her life. It was such a cliché she'd almost laughed in the fortune-teller's face. Certainly she didn't believe any part of the peculiar little woman's mumbo jumbo.

No more than she believed Jack was back in Galveston for good. She'd given him two weeks. In fact, it would probably take less before he started craving more revelry than the island's slow pace offered. In the meantime he'd made it clear that for as long as he did stay, he would do so under her roof. *Cohabit.* The very word made her tremble with repressed longings.

"I've no idea what's on your agenda, but I have a standing appointment with the lawn mower."

He helped himself to a glass of juice and a blueberry muffin before plopping down across the breakfast table from her. "You cut the grass every Saturday?"

"Somebody has to do it."

"Seems like that ought to be Clint's job."

"If I depended on my brother to take care of the yard, all the shrubs would be trees and the grass would have gone to seed." He'd neglected to put on a shirt again. The placement of each individual hair on his chest riveted her until she caught herself staring. "Oh, he professes to be interested in this place and its history, but I think he's really a closet condo man."

"Still, if he's going to live here, he has some responsibilities."

Jack as a crusader for domestic equality didn't compute. "Don't tell me you're stuck in the old man's-work–woman's-work time warp. Catch up, Rowland. This is the nineties."

"Please. It's too early for feminist rhetoric. Until I've had a massive jolt of caffeine, I'm in no condition to argue anything."

"You'll have to fend for yourself there. I drink only decaf tea."

He groaned. "Why doesn't that surprise me? You always were a little different from the rest of us mortals."

As if she needed Jack Rowland to point that out. Karolyn thought she had conquered the majority of her childhood insecurities, but he brought them roaring back like a storm surge. She wished it were Monday so she could escape to the lab. Except that her job no longer represented the haven she had withdrawn to in the past.

Great-Aunt Sadie's superstition about disasters coming in threes popped into her head. First the dilemma at work, now Jack. "What next?" she whispered ruefully.

Being a pragmatist, she had to deal with the most immediate problem. Jack. During the restless, endless hours between midnight and dawn, she'd come up with a compromise he might accept. "You know, Clint and I don't share the house. Technically."

"In my experience when someone uses the word 'technically,' they're trying to jerk me around."

Karolyn leaped to her feet, as if it were vital she rinse her plate and glass that very moment. "No, really, on the rare occasions he's home, I don't see all that much of him. He lives out in the original detached kitchen. Comes and goes as he pleases. My parents converted it into guest quarters not long after the two of you went off to Purdue."

"Okay, so you and your brother aren't housemates." He cocked a brow for emphasis. "Technically. What's the point?"

Very precisely she arranged her dishes in the dishwasher. "I just thought you would appreciate having . . . privacy. That way I won't disturb you."

"You don't disturb me, Kary." The heavy silence impelled her to turn around. His dark blue eyes drew her, enthralled her. "Does my being close disturb you?"

"No!" She practically shouted the lie, the second one he'd pressured her into telling. Luckily he hadn't pinned her to the wall about that secret-admirer nonsense or she'd have had to compound her original sin with still more deception. "I was only thinking of convenience."

"There's no reason to air-condition both in this heat wave. It's plenty convenient for me to stay right where I am in Clint's old bedroom."

Easy for him to say. After a single night, she was finding it terribly *in*convenient. But she sensed that he would have a counter for every argument. The man refused to be evicted. "As you wish," she conceded stiffly. In contests where brains counted, she usually won. Playing the graceful loser was foreign. "Just remember I tried to warn you."

"Your warning is duly noted. Now show me where the mower is so I can start earning my room and board."

Karolyn was extremely conscious of his following close behind as she led him to the garage. She was conscious, too, that her jonquil-yellow shorts and cropped red tank top were very revealing. Under normal circumstances she wouldn't have expected him to notice. But several times since yesterday afternoon she'd caught him watching her with what she had dubbed "The Look," something in his eyes and the hint of a smile that made her skin feel allover tingly.

The old Lawn Boy backfired, sputtered, and

bombed them with smoke, yet started more readily than it ever did for her. Whistling, he pushed it down the brick driveway, as if he couldn't wait to get on with his task. She predicted he would soon change his tune. The thermometer already read ninety-two in the shade.

There was a thought. Maybe if she assigned him a list of household chores, he'd tire of the boring routine and head for someplace more hospitable. Maybe, but not likely. Jack had always stubbornly resisted all attempts to manipulate him. He did pretty much as he pleased and to hell with anyone who didn't like it.

Ironically his devil-may-care attitude had made him enormously popular, especially with the opposite sex.

While he cut and edged the front, she fed the azaleas and hibiscus in back. When he returned to do the rear, she found a broom and bustled off to sweep the front walks. Despite the mower's noisy clatter, she heard him chuckle.

Karolyn prolonged the task as much as possible, but grew impatient pushing around the same pile of leaves and grass clippings. There wasn't any way to avoid him indefinitely, so she bent to scoop them into a trash can and almost took a header when she heard Jack clear his throat. Standing less than three feet away, he had sneaked up and caught her in a very undignified pose. Face flaming, she scrambled to right herself.

"Thought maybe you'd be ready for a drink by now." He held out a tall glass of ice water.

She grabbed the glass and gulped like a thirsty hound. The water didn't cool her off much, mainly because she couldn't focus on anything beyond his damp, bare chest and muscular legs. Didn't the man own any clothes other than shorts? And if he insisted on wearing them, why couldn't he have a repulsive paunch and be hairy as Pithecanthropus erectus? The nerve of him, looking good in sweat.

By comparison, she felt dirty, disheveled, and disheartened. She drained the glass, blaming the heat and humidity for short-circuiting her brain. Lustful urges were as alien to her as snow in Galveston. Doubly distressing was the fact that apparently Jack was the one male able to inspire them.

She dropped to her knees to scrape up the remaining clippings. "I have to run this over to—"

"Good morning, Karolyn," Mrs. Potter said, entering on cue. "I see your weekly offering to my compost pile is ready. It's cooking nicely in this heat. Come fall, we should have lots of lovely mulch."

"Hello, Mrs. Potter," Jack put in. "Remember me?"

"I may be old, Jack Rowland, but my memory isn't so impaired that I'm likely to forget a rascal like you. I'll declare, I thought we'd seen the last of you around these parts."

"Guess I'm like a bad penny." His unrepentant grin showed off perfect white teeth, another reason Karolyn could easily resent him. Unlike her, he hadn't had to suffer the ordeal of braces to get them. He gestured toward the house next door. "I see you're still growing roses."

"No thanks to you and Clint. Heaven knows I had to chase the two of you out of my flower beds often enough." She spoke to him in her sternest ex-teacher's voice, but her eyes sparkled with amused tolerance. Another conquest.

Karolyn said, "Every time Dad had to discipline Jack and Clint for some mischief, he'd shake his head and lament that if that pair of practical jokers ever got around to channeling their energy and creativity into something constructive, they'd probably end up millionaires." She handed the bin of clippings to her neighbor. "He got to say it real often."

"Yep, he sure did," Jack agreed, showing not

a trace of remorse. "But you know, Mrs. Potter, as you get older one of the things you have to admit is that parents know what they're talking about a good percentage of the time."

She beamed at him. "Glory be! I can't believe my ears. Some of what we tried to teach you took hold."

"In some areas I was a slow learner."

"It's the end result that matters," Mrs. Potter announced with conviction. "Now, you young people will have to excuse me. The garden club is coming for lunch and I must get on with my preparations."

Jack watched the spry, elderly lady cross the lawn and disappear around the side of her house. Then he turned back to Karolyn. "I may have been a slow learner, but a whiz kid like you was smart enough to know the truth all along."

If he applied the word "smart" to her one more time, she was going to inflict serious bodily harm. "I've learned my share the hard way, like everyone else. Getting all A's does not automatically guarantee having all the answers."

He shrugged. "I guess not. But even as a little kid, you had these big, serious eyes that took in everything and took it seriously. Kind of like you were a wise old soul trapped in a child's body."

"What a crock," she said, then regretted the

impulse. There was nothing wrong with letting him think of her as deeper, more complex than she really was. It gave her a small, badly needed advantage.

Karolyn dusted her hands together and said briskly, "Well, that's it for today. I don't want to hold you up any longer. You must have better things than yard work to do on your . . . vacation."

"Not at all. In fact I was about to ask what you had planned for this afternoon. Thought maybe you wouldn't mind my tagging along."

Darn! He was going to stick to her like beggar's-lice. Playing social director for Jack Rowland was not her idea of a relaxing time. Two weeks would be an eternity unless she found some way to tranquilize the rabble of butterflies in her stomach.

"Oh, I'm not doing anything special. Just the usual weekend errands. Boring stuff, I'm afraid."

"I don't mind. Let's get cleaned up and I'll treat you to lunch at Gaido's. Wanna race to see who's first in the shower?"

"Be my guest, please," she said with only a trace of sarcasm. Two weeks of sharing a bathroom. Was there a word for longer than eternity?

In reality she had only three errands, which required fewer than thirty minutes. Lunch had stretched on for a couple of hours because several people Jack had gone to school with stopped by their table to chat.

Karolyn experienced a flicker of hope each time anybody extended Jack an invitation. Those hopes died in turn when he remained frustratingly noncommittal about accepting even one. He exchanged phone numbers and promised they would get together, but refused to be pinned down to specifics.

She pasted on a smile when Jack introduced her, and did her best to be pleasant. It wasn't easy, given the speculative looks directed at her. She could read their thoughts—surely Jack Rowland wasn't romantically involved with someone like Karolyn Lucas. She wasn't his type.

When they finally left Gaido's, it was mid-afternoon. The pavement sizzled hot enough to scorch the soles of her sandals. Across Seawall Boulevard on the beach, sun worshipers basted themselves with oil and stretched out to be fried like a batch of hush puppies. What idiots to disregard scientific evidence for vanity's sake.

She glanced at Jack. His skin sported an all-over tan, or at least the parts she'd seen were tan. Though he'd dressed up in longer shorts and a polo shirt, her mind's eye saw him wearing considerably less. His hair and brows were sun-bleached and fine creases fanned out from the corners of his eyes. An ideal candidate for a lecture on the sun's ravages. But, as she was relearning, Jack paid scant attention to lectures of any kind.

"What's next?" he asked, catching her studying him.

All Karolyn really wanted to do was stop by the bookstore and pick up the latest release by her favorite Regency-romance novelist, then curl up in air-conditioned comfort to enjoy one of her guilty pleasures. She could imagine her newly acquired shadow's reaction to that.

"The Sandcastle Competition is at Apffel Park today. Want to check it out?" Braving the fires of Hades was preferable to cooping herself up in the house with Jack.

"Sounds good. What is it?"

"A bunch of architects get together and see who can come up with the most original design. They started about six years ago and each one attracts a bigger crowd."

"Seems like there's more going on here all the time than I remember."

"During the eighties, the Convention and Visitors Bureau launched an aggressive marketing campaign to attract tourists. In some ways I think it's been too successful. There are times when the natives have to flee the island or be overtaken by outsiders."

"Where do *you* flee?"

"Oh, usually up to Houston for the weekend, though that hardly qualifies as peace and quiet. It's a different sort of chaos. I'm always relieved to come home."

His hand cupped her elbow as they walked across the parking lot to his car. Karolyn jumped at the pulsing warmth and energy of the contact. He let go to walk around to his side, but long after he'd pointed the car toward the eastern end of the island, a residual tingling remained.

"Clint told me about some of the job offers you turned down. They sounded pretty impressive. Huge pharmaceutical companies, well-known hospitals, the CDC in Atlanta, National Institutes of Health. Yet you chose to come back to Galveston and do research. Why?"

"It's simple, really. From the time I hit middle school, I went off every summer to participate in some accelerated academic program or camp or retreat. Then I spent the better part of seven years at college and graduate school. None of those places ever felt quite right. About three years ago it came to me that I'd been away from home long enough." Too late she realized she had more or less echoed his own sentiments.

"I know exactly how you feel. It just took me a little longer. But then, nobody ever accused me of being as quick a study as you."

"Let's see if you're quick enough to understand that I will forget the rug beater and go after you with that chunk of iron if you make one more joke about my intelligence."

His mouth dropped open in astonishment. "Your intelligence is no joke, Kary. It's awesome, and I respect it. Always have."

He sounded so sincere that it was her turn to be astonished. Did she dare believe him? "Talk is cheap. I've heard lots of men claim to value intelligence in a woman. The reality is, most of them are intimidated and threatened by too much of it."

"You've obviously been hanging around the wrong men." His self-assured grin told its own tale. Jack would never be threatened by anything about any woman.

"I don't hang around men much at all." She gritted her teeth when his grin widened.

He pulled into the park and paid the admission fee. "Now that you've acquired a secret admirer, I expect that will change. Sooner or later he'll reveal himself and things are bound to heat up then."

"It won't amount to anything." Though she

sounded adamant, she heard the underlying quiver of longing in her voice and feared he had heard it too. She couldn't scramble out of the car fast enough.

He caught up with her quickly. Hooking his finger through the straps of the sandals she had kicked off, he fell into step beside her. "On the other hand, you have to admit it has interesting possibilities. Risking the unknown always heightens the excitement."

The quiver shot straight to her stomach. "That's great for fairy tales. It doesn't happen in real life." Except to other women.

"You're too skeptical, Kary. Goes along with being a scientist, I guess. Never believe in anything you can't see or touch is how that works, right?"

"I like to see evidence." They passed by crews armed with wheelbarrows, buckets, sculpting tools, and rakes. Teams of builders swarmed around the wooden forms they had constructed for their designs.

"Isn't it true that evidence sometimes leads to wrong conclusions?"

"Look over there!" she exclaimed, ignoring his cryptic question. "Guy must be crazy from the heat."

Disregarding the soaring temperatures, "Batman" in a mask and swirling ankle-length cape swept up to warn them. "Beware! Catwoman lurks nearby." Sure enough, on the opposite side of the "Batmobile," a bas-relief replica molded in dark sand, a willowy woman in a black catsuit swayed sinuously and posed seductively, beckoning to Jack.

He laughed, but shook his head and tugged Karolyn toward the next sculpture. Stunned, she bit her tongue to keep from blurting out the obvious question. Since when did Jack start passing up the chance to charm a willing female? Was it possible he'd changed so drastically? No, that was too much to hope for.

Wait a minute. She was getting way too mixed up in matters that didn't concern her. Karolyn forced herself to concentrate on the display, an impressive pyramid with the face of Elvis carved into one side.

"These people take the game seriously, don't they?" he asked. The crew was pumping water out of the Gulf to spray down their hero's likeness.

She was tempted to wrest the sprayer away and turn it on herself. "If they don't keep them wet, their works of art will crumble before the judges make their rounds."

"So it really is a competition?"

"Oh, yes." She glanced up at him, saw the tiny beads of moisture dotting his face and neck, and wondered how she could inconspicuously blot the trickle that ran between her breasts. "They're all out to win the Golden Bucket Award."

Jack took off his sunglasses, hypnotizing her with the dark power of his eyes. "I know how they feel. I want to win too. So badly that I'll do whatever it takes."

How could she be so hot, yet feel a chill slither up her spine? She yearned to ask him what he wanted to win so badly, but kept the question inside. It had nothing to do with her. "Look at the detail in this one."

Jack took only a few seconds to study the intricate design of a trash can dumping on a sunken earth that was connected to a recycling center, which then led to a resurgent whole earth. "So you've been back, what, three years?"

"Almost."

"Ever think about venturing out again, maybe taking one of those prestigious jobs to make a name for yourself?"

"My name's just fine as it is," she said defensively. He was getting a little too close. "I'm happy right where I am. This may be hard for you to grasp, but not everybody is consumed with wanderlust. Some of us actually want to stay put except for an occasional vacation."

"Where'd you go on your last vacation?"

"I used it to move into my parents' house." Karolyn took off down the beach, kicking up sand. Because men seldom asked about details of her personal life, his sudden interest made her uncomfortable.

A few large strides and he drew even with her. "That's right. Clint told me when your dad took the sabbatical to England, you gave up your place to move in and house-sit. Where was it?"

"Where was what?"

"Your place."

"Oh. In the Texas Christian Advocate Building down on Mechanic. It had been used as the rigging loft during the restoration of the tall ship *Elissa*. Then it was adapted for reuse and I leased one of the second-floor apartments over a gallery." Good grief. She sounded like a guide on the Historic Homes Tour.

He didn't appear as bored as she'd have expected. "That put you real close to UTMB," he said, referring to the University of Texas Medical Branch. "Did you walk to work?"

Every time he spoke, he edged a little closer. "Bike," she said, growing more agitated with each question. "Anything else you want to know, like maybe my bra size?" She felt herself turn red faster than crabs in a steamer.

His lips curved into a smile, slow and sexy and knowing. Then he dropped his gaze, as if he were taking her measurements. "Sure, Kary. I'm interested in finding out every last thing there is to know about you."

Seconds passed, counted by double beats of her heart. He stood so near she could feel his heat, smell it. She heard herself swallow and knew that he did too. At last he said, "Where to now?"

She licked her lips, caught herself, and wiped them with her palm. Batman wasn't the only one crazy from the heat. "I've had enough for one day." Karolyn tightened the rein on her jumbled senses, threw back her shoulders, and marched off again.

Jack let her gain some distance, and time to calm down. He didn't want her so flustered she'd refuse to talk to him. Or worse, try to kick him out of the house again. Proximity was essential to his plans.

"Damn!" Only the second day and he was already moving too fast, trying to force her to catch up with him. He supposed it was selfish, but now that he'd made the decision to settle down here for good, he wanted proof positive that Kary would be content to remain alongside him. So he'd badgered her, and she had retreated.

When he saw that she had almost reached the car, Jack sprinted to catch up. "Better wait until you put these on." He bent to place the sandals so she could slip into them, and noticed that her feet were slim and high-arched, her toenails painted a pale, pearly pink. He stood up quickly, fighting the temptation to touch. "Come on. I think we've earned something tall and cool. You name the place."

Much later that night, Jack flopped from his stomach to his back for the twenty-seventh time. Twenty-seven, that was, since he'd started counting. He had to do something to keep his mind off the fact that only a pair of pocket doors separated him from Kary and her bed.

He had told her being close didn't disturb him. In a way that was true because he did want them to spend as much time together as possible. In another sense, today had been torture. He'd tried to be so careful about everything he said or did that he hadn't been able to relax and have fun.

Maybe he was approaching this courtship strategy all wrong. Aside from the way she felt about him, he had no desire to change Kary.

Didn't it follow that he shouldn't try to change himself either? His feelings were honest, his intentions honorable. Why should he bend over backward to turn himself into somebody she might fall for? Sooner or later she would have to live with the real Jack, warts and all. Better for her to accept that up front.

Fighting the tangled sheets, he turned on his side to stare out the arched window onto the front upstairs gallery. Many a night when he and Clint had been kids they had crept out there to climb down the huge slanted walnut tree and roam the neighborhood till the wee hours. They'd never done a thing that they couldn't have done any other time. But sneaking away undetected had satisfied their boyish thirst for adventure.

Without consciously deciding to, he rolled from the bed, pulled on the shorts he'd discarded earlier, and inch by inch eased up the tall walk-through window.

As he was about to step out, Kary half turned from her post at the railing and said softly, "No need to skulk. I beat you to the punch."

"What are you doing out here?" His own voice sounded hoarse, not surprising because her white robe came only to midthigh and it was lightweight and sheer enough to create some very interesting shadows in the moonlight.

"Did you think you and Clint were the only ones who'd caught on to this little secret?"

"I just never pictured you as the tree-climbing type."

"I know exactly how you picture me." She folded her arms at her waist and turned back to face the street. "But you never have looked close enough to see all of me."

He wanted to agree, then tell her that from now on everything would be different, that he couldn't wait to see and know everything. But since she'd whispered the last part, he figured she hadn't meant him to hear. So he pretended he hadn't. "Do you do this often? Come out here by yourself late at night?"

"Hardly ever, anymore. I used to a lot when I was a teenager. Not to climb down, though. Just to think."

About what? he wondered. "Why tonight?"

"I couldn't sleep. The air-conditioning is practically useless upstairs when it's this hot. And all the ceiling fan does is stir around the hot air." With one hand she lifted her loosely braided hair off her neck, and used the other to fan the skin she'd exposed.

Desperately Jack looked around for something he could do to prevent himself from kissing her there. He pulled one of the padded wicker chairs forward, sat, and propped his ankles on the railing. "It's no cooler out here."

"I know. But I felt so . . . confined in there."

"I know." Hot or not, he definitely preferred being outside. Reaching back, he snagged the arm of another chair and brought it even with his.

She murmured, "Thank you," and sort of tumbled into it, as if she had suddenly needed the support.

Making small talk with the opposite sex had always been easy—almost instinctive—for Jack. At this moment his mouth might as well have been glued shut. So they sat there for a long time without speaking, and pretty soon the silence started to feel okay. Kind of nice, in fact. He let out a deep sigh and relaxed. Yep, sharing quiet time with Kary was all right. It could become a habit.

"Jack?"

"Um-hmm?"

"Remember the day you beat up Chuck Goff?"

"I remember." His lids had drifted shut, but he lifted them and pointed across the street. "Pounded him in the ground right over there."

"He'd yanked off my glasses and was running

around me in circles singing, 'Four eyes, four eyes, bet you can't see me now with no eyes.'"

His chest tightened. After all these years, he could still feel the fury welling up in him that someone had dared taunt Kary that way. "Chuck Goff was a bully."

"Yes. And after you bloodied his nose and gave him a shiner, you kicked him all the way to the corner and told him you never wanted to see him on P 1/2 Street again."

"He had it coming. His kind always does."

"Even when your father grounded you for fighting, you didn't protest at all. Clint told me."

"Sometimes breaking the rules is more important than suffering the punishment."

Again they lapsed into silence until she asked, "I don't suppose you remember what I called you afterward."

Jack flattened his palm on his chest where his heart had begun to pound heavily. "You called me your hero."

"Yes, and I meant it. At that moment you were my Prince Charming."

He laid his hand very lightly atop hers. "What would it take for you to see me that way again, Kary?"

THREE

"You have a *man* living in your house!"

"Shh. Keep your voice down. You know how easy it is to set the grapevine abuzz." Karolyn was having lunch in one of the hospital cafeterias with her best friend. Pepper had left for a vacation in Cancún when Karolyn returned from her own trip a week ago. Both had faced a backlog of work, so Friday noon was the first chance they'd had to catch up.

"Shame on you for holding out on me, Karo. I didn't know you were seeing a man, much less thinking about asking one to move in."

"Don't jump to conclusions." While Pepper picked at her tuna-stuffed tomato Karolyn explained the situation. "So you see, it isn't as if we're really *living* together." Jack had called it cohabiting, which sounded even more intimate.

"Plus, I'm sure he won't be hanging around for as long as he thinks."

"One can accomplish miracles in a short time if properly motivated." Pepper's dark eyes sparkled with merriment. "Is he good-looking? Rich? Available?" When Karolyn shot her friend a give-me-a-break look, she giggled and said, "A simple answer to all of the above, please."

"Oh, all right. Yes. I don't know. I don't know."

"Well, that last 'I don't know' could be a problem. Why don't you ask him?"

"Ask if he's available?" Karolyn contemplated the black olive she'd speared from her Greek salad. "Why would I want to do that?"

"How can someone so brilliant be so obtuse in certain areas?" No one ever called Pepper subtle. "You ask in order to find out if you have a chance to snag him."

"I can tell you that right now. If—notice I said *if*—I were interested in him that way, it wouldn't do me any good. I've known Jack Rowland for as long as I can remember, and I am not his type."

"Who is?"

"Perky, petite blondes. The kind who've elevated simpering to an art form, and who can gaze adoringly at jocks for hours at a time. Not real high-wattage IQs, but nobody notices because they are champion smilers."

Pepper burst out laughing. "Too bad you weren't sufficiently interested to do an extensive study."

Karolyn bristled at the implication. "I didn't have to do a study. It was right there under my nose. Clint and Jack were inseparable, so girls were constantly calling our house for 'Ja-a-ck,' and they camped out around there like rock-star groupies hoping for backstage passes."

"I've seen your brother and he *is* something to behold. If Jack is half as cinchy, he's a prize." In cases where Pepper didn't like the current slang, she created her own words.

"You wouldn't be so enamored if you'd had to endure them when you were growing up. They were unbelievably, obnoxiously cocky, both world-class pains in the tush."

"But you're all adults now. You and Clint are pretty tight. Any reason you can't get along equally well with Jack?"

No reason except that being around the man kept her off balance, as she'd been late Saturday night when he'd asked what it would take for her to see him as her hero again. She'd stammered, hedged, and finally tried to turn it into a joke.

Neither of them had laughed. Nor was she able to get his unexpected question off her mind.

"Jack is . . . well, Jack. And my feelings about him are as ambivalent as they were years ago." But with his return, the ambivalence frequently gave way to a keen awareness of him as a man.

"What does that mean?"

"Even though he irritated me no end and I considered him an adversary, deep down I recognized that to others he was cute and athletic, confident and popular."

"Ah, I get it. In short, he was everything you weren't."

"And never will be."

"Come on, Karo. Don't get mired down in your shortcomings again. Most of them are in your head and those that aren't can be changed."

"Right," Karolyn said dryly. "You're going to wave your magic wand and turn me into the homecoming queen." She truly didn't aspire to anything that trivial. But she often wished she could swim more easily in the mainstream.

"No wand. Just me preaching that if you want more than you have, why not go for it?"

Their conversations frequently led around to this subject. Ever since she had confessed to a general malaise pervading her life, Pepper had been badgering her to take action. Trouble was, Karolyn couldn't quite pin down the cause of her discontent. Science, not self-analysis, was her forte.

"I took your advice and got rid of my thick glasses." They both knew her switch to contact lenses was more than a symbolic first step. It was a commitment to change.

"So you did. What's next? Going to interview for that assistant professorship in molecular biology?"

Her stomach revolted at the prospect of a career change. She understood the subject as thoroughly as anybody on staff, which didn't mean she could handle the transition from research to lecturing and dealing with students on a daily basis. The crucial decision had to be made soon, but every time she envisioned leaving the security of her lab, it brought on a panic attack. So she procrastinated.

"I have a feeling that surviving a couple of weeks with Jack underfoot will be enough of a challenge. Once he's gone, maybe I can come to some decision about the new position."

"But didn't he say he's here to stay?"

"He did. I just don't believe it. A man who's spent the past twelve years chasing one foreign contract after another, from the Mid East to the

North Sea to God knows where in Asia does not suddenly wake up one day and announce, 'I think I'll settle down in Galveston, Texas.'"

"I don't see why not." Pepper crumpled her napkin and reached for her purse. "Basically that's what you did."

"It isn't the same thing at all," Karolyn protested. Her life was built around routine and stability, but this whole business had her so confused she wasn't thinking rationally. On the one hand getting Jack out of her house had monopolized her thoughts. On the other she dreaded the day she would go home and find that he'd taken off, never to be seen or heard from again. "Oh, what does it matter anyway?"

She stood and gathered up her wallet and a file folder. "I can't believe we spent the whole time discussing what's going on with me. I wanted to hear all about Mexico."

"In a word, stupendous. I'm picking up my pictures this afternoon. Maybe we can get together over the weekend and I'll bore you with the complete travelogue. Unless, of course, you have plans with Jack."

"No. I'm sure he will have found someone more, uh, worthwhile to spend time with. I'll give you a call." Outside the cafeteria they set off in opposite directions; Pepper to her job in human relations, Karolyn to the sanctuary of the lab.

She entered the building and immediately the receptionist called to her. "Karolyn, here. This was delivered while you were gone."

"Must be that report I reques—" She halted, stunned by the simple beauty of a cut-glass bowl in which a single exotic blossom floated.

"I've signed for a few dozen roses, balloon bouquets, kittens, even a box of chocolate condoms," the receptionist said, blushing. "But never anything like this." Her gray head bobbed and she beamed up at Karolyn. "It's so elegant, and so . . . romantic. Hurry! Read the card."

As if it might contain a serpent ready to strike, Karolyn held the envelope by its corner, cautiously thumbed open the flap, and extracted an ivory card. The message, scripted in calligraphy, read: *This is a Pearl Harbor, one of the rarest and most beautiful of all orchids. It can't compare with you.* She read the signature aloud. "Your Secret Admirer."

Karolyn moaned and sank into the closest chair. Disaster number three had struck. She'd gone insane!

To impress Jack, she had fabricated a man who didn't exist, and this was her punishment— delusions that the imaginary man really had sent her a gift. She saw her hands shake as they wrapped around the bowl. It felt cool, sharply etched, and when she lifted it, very heavy. Hardly the product of a deranged mind. "Who brought this?"

"One of the regular delivery services."

"Which one? I have to know."

"Well, I'm not sure. We get so many every day. The doctors request material from all over the place. I lose track of what comes from where."

Heart pounding, Karolyn cupped the bowl and brought it closer. The orchid was delicate, exquisite, and he had said it didn't compare with her. The faintest of scents drifted upward and she closed her eyes, swaying slightly. Nothing like this had ever happened to her, and she didn't understand why it was happening now.

She was not so naive as to believe that wishing hard enough for something would make it come true, but every other explanation was equally implausible. She was more confused than ever.

What kind of man would compare a socially backward bookworm like Karolyn Lucas to a rare and lovely blossom?

That same question was still uppermost in her mind when she left the lab around six. She had swiped a heavy towel to use as padding so the crystal bowl wouldn't slide around in her bike basket, but she still took extra care pedaling home. Hoping to elude Jack long enough to sneak the flower up to her room, she parked the bike out front instead of taking it back to the garage.

"Hi, Kary," he said the second she opened the door. He was wearing jeans and a navy polo shirt that matched his eyes. Had he dressed up to go out? "How'd your day go?"

"Fine, fine." She furtively rearranged the towel to conceal the bowl. "A typical day in the lab. Nothing out of the ordinary. I hope yours was as, uh, normal as mine." Now he had her babbling and lying in the same breath.

"Can't say it was exactly normal. I watched nonstop talk shows, six of 'em."

"May I be the first to commend you? It takes real fortitude to survive a whole day of geek-a-thons."

"TV has changed some since I last had a steady diet of it. But I did learn some fascinating stuff. It started out pretty tame, with how to teach a man to do household chores. Next came dangers of cheerleading, followed by the doctor who claimed a rat told him to murder his wife."

"Fascinating stuff, all right," she agreed, deadpan.

"There's more. For instance, did you know thousands of happily married women carry on affairs? Or that interracial homosexual couples have lots of problems?" He squinted, appearing thoughtful. "I guess my favorite was the one where they interviewed male virgins."

"Why? I'm sure you deserted the ranks long ago." He laughed, a low, evocative sound that vibrated in her stomach. She inhaled deeply and held for a count of five. It didn't help. "Well, I'm glad you were able to spend the day relaxing."

"I remembered what they said on Geraldo and squeezed in a few chores too." He held up a spray can of WD-40. "A bunch of the doors around here are squeaky, so I'm giving them a shot of this."

"How very . . . handy of you." Karolyn tried to sidle past him and at the same time keep her bundle out of sight.

"Whatcha got there? A goldfish bowl?" Despite her evasive tactics, he unraveled the towel. "Uh-oh. The secret admirer strikes again. Guy's fixated on flowers, isn't he? What is that thing, a spider lily?"

"A Pearl Harbor," she told him huffily. "The rarest and most beautiful orchid in the world."

"Pardon me. I stand corrected." He bent and took a couple of loud sniffs. "Not much smell. And how come he didn't send a whole vase of them? Kinda chintzy on his part, if you ask me."

"No one asked you." Jack and his little digs put her in the position of defending a phantom, or else someone who was in all likelihood playing a practical joke on her. All afternoon she'd worried the question like a sore tooth. Who? "I think it's lovely and . . . and perfect."

She flounced up the steps, but he dogged her heels. "I can't believe you women are such suckers for all that drivel. Next thing you know he'll be writing flowery poems and sending candy in a heart-shaped box. Talk about dopey."

At the door to her room Karolyn turned on him, incensed. "Just because you're too boorish and muleheaded to appreciate the beauty of a romantic gesture doesn't give you license to ridicule someone who's sweet and sentimental and sensitive."

"Sensitive, huh? Is that a ten-dollar word for wimpy?"

"Just get out of my face, Jack Rowland." She whirled and slammed the door on his sardonic smile.

Arranging the bowl in a place of honor, she muttered to herself, "Two and a half billion men on the planet and I have to get stuck with the most maddening of them all, not to mention the most blatantly masculine. You're going to owe me for this one, big brother."

She coiled her long braid into a knot and secured it with several tortoiseshell pins. Five minutes spent with Jack had gotten her hot under the collar.

At that moment she noticed the neat stacks of clothes on her bed. She marched over, and when what he'd done sank in, she saw red. Three giant steps and she flung open the door. Jack was squirting oil on the door hinges of his room. *Clint's room.*

"You did the laundry!" Her accusation rang as shrill as a fishwife's.

Elbows framing his waist, he put out his hands palms up. She supposed it was his rendition of an "Aw shucks ma'am, 'twern't nothin'" pose. "And they say TV isn't educational."

"But you—"

"Sorry about turning all your white things lavender. Guess I shouldn't have thrown in my purple shorts, eh?"

"You did my *underwear*!"

"Well, yeah," he said matter-of-factly. "I did everything that was in the basket in the hall closet. I remember your mom's house rule. You want it washed, it better be in the basket."

She suppressed the urge to stomp her foot and yell at him. That would be a juvenile overreaction. So what if he had seen her underwear, touched it? He'd probably seen and touched so much fancy female lingerie that her plain white cotton wouldn't even register.

"Oh," he said, that damnably devilish smile spreading. "I get it. You don't like anybody messing with your unmentionables."

"I don't like anybody messing with me, period."

"Don't worry, Kary. I'm not real kinky. If I want to feel a woman's slip or bra or panties, you can bet she'll be wearing them, and wanting the same thing."

A sudden burst of heat inundated her. Her whole body turned damp and feverish. A muted whimper escaped her throat. It simply was not fair. One minute he had her shrieking, the next he made her pulse with a sensual longing so acute it stole her breath.

Mustering as much dignity as she could, Karolyn sought cover in her room, behind a locked door. "In your dreams." No, no! She *couldn't* have said that aloud.

And he *could not* have replied, "You got that right."

She grasped one of the pineapple finials on her old iron-pipe bed, as if it could tether her to reality. Books and collectibles from her childhood, as well as some that reflected recently acquired interests, cluttered the room. But today she found no solace in the familiar.

Instead it was the orchid that commanded her attention. How ironic that something so flawless should symbolize the turmoil swirling around her. She hadn't asked for any of it, wished it all would evaporate as quickly as it had appeared. She didn't need Jack and his confounding intrusion in her life. Or the mysterious secret admirer who had seemingly materialized from her fertile imagination.

Or had he? That was the crux of the problem. Who was behind this scenario, and why? She'd considered and discarded half the males she knew. There were dozens of candidates, but none of them had ever expressed any romantic interest in her.

Two sharp raps on the door jerked her from her muddled musings. "Come on down when you're ready, Kary. I have dinner in the oven. Roast beef à la Geraldo." She heard his bare feet slapping on the pine-planked floor.

When she was sure he'd gone downstairs, she rushed to the bathroom and doused her face with cold water. Then she stowed the evidence of Jack's very male presence in a cupboard.

This was her home and, by heaven, no itinerant rogue was going to distract her with his razor, his hairbrush, his after-shave, or his sexy innuendoes. She was in charge here and it was past time to assert herself. Although she hadn't succeeded in deposing him, she could certainly call a halt to all this togetherness.

In the week since she'd returned, she didn't think he had ventured off the property without her, except to grocery-shop for their shared meals. Which ought to make him primed for a diversion. And she had the perfect candidate in mind. But maybe she'd postpone bringing it up until after they'd eaten. She was ravenous. No need to disrupt dinner.

One could only hope he possessed more expertise in the kitchen than he had in the utility room. Still, she had to admit she found his Mr. Mom attempts rather endearing. "Forget that," she whispered. "Leave it to other women to admire his dubious charms. I am immune." Maybe if she repeated that often enough, she'd start believing it.

Fortified, she descended the steps and approached the kitchen with only the tiniest bit of trepidation.

Karolyn found him eyeing the roasting pan askance. "I don't think this meat looks the way it's supposed to, do you? And it smells kind of . . . raw. I remember being able to smell your mom's roast all over the house."

She leaned around him to get a look. He'd selected a large rump cut, but rather than being nicely browned and juicy, it had turned a sickly taupe. "How much does this weigh?"

He shrugged. "Beats me. Is that important?"

"It helps. How long did you leave it in the oven?"

"Twenty minutes. That's what they said on the cooking demonstration."

"I think they probably said twenty minutes per *pound*. In which case, this is underdone by at least an hour."

"Oh," he said, visibly deflated. "Guess I didn't listen closely enough." He stood there, clearly unsure about how to proceed.

"Since you just took it out, there's no harm in sticking it back in for the remaining time." Stomach growling, she whisked the pan back into the oven and checked the clock and temperature setting. "We'll give it an hour."

Jack slumped in a chair. "You've cooked all week. I wanted to surprise you by having dinner ready tonight. Kind of an Andy and Aunt Bea role reversal. I even bought a pie at the bakery." He appeared to her like a little boy lost and dejected.

Resisting the urge to laugh, Karolyn weakened, telling herself she was a fool. "I'm not that hungry yet anyway. Why don't you pour us a glass of wine and we'll take it out on the porch? Hard to believe, but a cool front moved through this afternoon. It's really quite pleasant."

"Good idea." He perked up amazingly fast. "You go on and get comfortable. I'll bring the wine."

He followed her a few minutes later, bearing a tray that held an uncorked bottle of fumé blanc, a round of cheese, and a sliced pear. After filling their glasses, he sat beside her in the glider and proposed a simple toast. "To the future."

He said it with such intent, Karolyn's fingers tightened on the stem, but she bravely echoed his toast. Just as they touched glasses an annoying female voice trilled, "Ja-a-ck Rowland! Is that really ye-ew? I don't believe my eyes."

"Doesn't believe her eyes, my foot," Karolyn grumbled under her breath. "Her radar probably locked on target the minute you crossed the county line."

"Hello, Tammy. How are you?" Jack obviously recognized her and responded politely, but he didn't sound overjoyed by the blonde's appearance.

"Super, just super," Tammy bubbled, hips asway as she minced up the sidewalk in shocking-pink spandex bike shorts under what looked like a tutu. "I don't have to ask how you are. You look great, terrific. As always."

And you look predatory. As always. "Hi there, Tammy," Karolyn chirped in a close approximation of the other woman's voice. "I'm just super too."

Tammy narrowed her eyes and said, "Hello . . . Karolyn, isn't it? Clint's baby sister?"

"Congratulations. Your memory is as great and terrific as Jack looks. How are your three children? Or is it four?"

Jack cleared his throat. "You used to live on Jamaica Beach, didn't you? What brings you to this part of town?"

"The scent of male flesh," Karolyn whispered out the corner of her mouth. That earned her a stern glare, but his lips twitched.

Tammy patted her big hair and puffed out her impressive chest for inspection, a feat easily accomplished thanks to her skimpy halter top. "Oh, I'm doing my daily exercise. I walk a couple of miles every evening. Today I decided to vary my route a little. Imagine my surprise, running into you. How long will you be here?"

The glider shook as Jack angled his body toward Karolyn. "I've decided to stay for good."

Tammy licked her lips; Karolyn felt like snarling. "Why that's wonderful news! I'm having a little get-together tomorrow night at my place. Stop by and I can guarantee you'll have fun."

A little get-together for two, no doubt. Bet I can guess your idea of fun.

"Thanks for the invitation, but Kary and I already have plans."

We do? Here's your chance, dummy. Gloat. "That's right, we do," she confirmed, trying her best to look smug. "Maybe another time. Right now you'll have to excuse us. Jack cooked me dinner and it's waiting." She stood and beckoned for him to come along. He—to his credit— readily obeyed. Maybe there was hope for the man.

"Shame on you," he said once they were inside. "I had no idea you harbored a latent catty streak behind that brainy exterior."

"I thought I was the soul of discretion. Did I say a word about the twenty-odd extra pounds she's packing? Or which divorce she's currently working on? And how about the outfit that looked like it's off the rack from Tarts-R-Us?"

He locked the door and turned to face her. "If I didn't see you as above that sort of thing, the word 'jealous' would come to mind."

"Jealous!" she sputtered, unwilling to admit

that he'd zeroed in on the reason for her shrewish behavior. "Me? Of that vapid, varnish-haired vamp?"

"Super alliteration, Kary. You always had a way with words."

"Oh, go suck an egg." Now, there was an articulate response. Fuming, she rifled through the mail on the hall table, though her mind centered on past offenses. "I guess I couldn't resist a payback." The envelopes slipped from her fingers. "Tammy Shifflet once tried to bribe me with a dirty, wadded-up dollar bill to tell her where you were, and with whom."

He cursed. "That's about her speed."

"At various times she also called me a retarded undernourished, bug-eyed, worthless little nuisance."

"I can imagine how you responded to that."

No, he couldn't. Not in a million years. Because he'd never been on the other side, one of the outcasts. "I should have abandoned you to her tender mercies." Forget dinner. She just wanted to hide out in her room.

"Why didn't you?"

That stopped her short on the bottom step. She turned and found him right behind her, looking into her eyes. She didn't owe him an explanation, but for some reason she needed to justify her performance. "Look, I understand that you're in the market for female companionship. I just think you can do better than a bleached, brazen bimbo."

"Got an alternative?"

Why was this so hard? "Yes. I have a friend. She isn't blond, but she does know how to have a good time. I think the two of you would . . . hit it off."

"Kary, why don't you let me take care of my own love life?" His index and middle fingers grazed her nose, her lips, her chin, coming to rest at the pulse point in the hollow of her throat. "I know what I want. And I know where to find it."

"You do?"

"Umm-hmm. Here, I'll show you."

FOUR

This couldn't be happening. Not to her, anyway.

Jack stood motionless, but Karolyn didn't have to guess what his next move would be. He was going to kiss her. She stood motionless, too, unable—or perhaps unwilling—to resist. Then he fitted his mouth to hers.

He took no further liberties, yet there was nothing weak or indecisive about the contact. His message was clear. He found the warmth, the shape, even the slight resistance of her lips special treats worth lingering over. His lack of haste seemed to say that the magic of a first kiss deserved to be savored slowly, and that he would be endlessly patient in order to ensure that she shared equally in the pleasure.

She closed her eyes, which only enhanced the gentle but firm pressure of his mouth. Because he invited her response rather than demanding it, the invitation proved to be a powerful seducer.

Karolyn parted her lips and, against his, felt the fierce rush of her own breath. He opened, and for a few seconds the moist heat blended, bathing her face. The sensation was so intense, she groped for the stair railing. Again, she felt hot all over, but shivery too. And . . . achy. How could he do this to her with a mere touch of his lips? It hardly even qualified as a real kiss and here she was, in danger of collapsing at his feet.

As a prepubescent girl she had somehow comprehended Jack's masculine appeal in the abstract. This was different. Tonight she experienced it as a palpable entity, a force that could consume her, body and mind. *If* she were fool enough to allow it. Karolyn Lucas was no fool.

She clambered up to the next step, giving herself the advantage of height and distance. "Why did you do that?"

"For all the usual reasons a man kisses a woman." He hooked both thumbs in his jeans pocket and tipped back his head to arrest her with those eyes. "Mostly I did it because I wanted to."

"Wanted to put me in my place, don't you mean?" The trace of indignation struck a nice note, she thought, relieved that the internal shaking hadn't spilled over into her voice. "I meddled in your little tête-à-tête outside and you couldn't let it go unpunished."

"Damn, Kary. You're hard on a man's ego. If that kiss came across as punishment, my technique must really need work."

"Ha! I'm so sure you're worried." When she couldn't stand the silence any longer, she relented. "I doubt you've heard many complaints about your technique from those hordes of other women." Let him presume that only she was discerning enough not to be affected. No telling what he'd do if he knew how deeply she'd been moved by his barely-there kiss.

"Hordes is a slight exaggeration."

"You know what I meant."

"Unfortunately I think I do." He rubbed his knuckles along his jawline. She tried to tune out the raspy sound and how it called to her senses. "But, Kary, there's one skill most men finally master after having known quite a few women."

How well she could imagine. "And that is?"

"They learn to tell the difference between gold and dross, and a smart man will never again mistake one for the other."

Did he speak from personal experience? Her chest was so constricted she had to force out the words. "How does that translate to what just happened?"

"You figure it out. I will give you a hint, though. Bear in mind who I kissed and who I turned away from without a backward glance."

He broke eye contact and headed toward the kitchen. "I'm going to put dinner on the table now, and don't even think about pleading the excuse that you're not hungry."

Karolyn's bottom hit the stair tread with a thump. She clung to a baluster with both hands, replaying every word, every nuance of Jack's last speech. After each conversation between them, she grew increasingly bewildered. She couldn't get a fix on his intentions or how she figured into them. It would be so easy to conclude he was playing with her, but what did he have to gain? He could dally with any woman he chose.

Granted, in the past Jack had teased her plenty. He hadn't, however, been genuinely nasty or malicious, as others had. She couldn't see him starting now. That still didn't explain why he'd kissed her. Should she confront him and ask? Act as though it never took place? Or pack a bag and run away?

For someone who habitually planned ahead, she hadn't the foggiest notion as to what her next move should be.

Karolyn heard the early-eighteenth-century long-case clock, her mother's pride and joy, chime four times. Repeatedly and with great determination, she had closed her eyes, but she had yet to fall asleep. Even several attempts to read had frustrated her.

She'd kept an ear trained for signs of similar restlessness next door, but apparently Jack was off to dreamland, untroubled by the kiss or the fact that he'd made bedlam of her life.

She could take consolation in the fact that she'd bluffed her way through dinner, several programs on the Discovery Channel, and the ten o'clock news. Never mind that she hadn't tasted a bite of food or retained a shred of what she'd watched. At least she had *appeared* unperturbed. Under the circumstances that was the best she could hope for.

Exhaustion finally claimed her before the clock struck again. But even her dreams were full of fitful, passionate writhings, so tempestuous, so hot, and so realistic, swelling and sharpening to a peak . . . just before she awoke with a start. Her nightshirt was drenched. She'd kicked all the covers off the bed. And deep inside, her body throbbed almost painfully.

At that moment the only thing she could focus on was calming down, cooling off, and getting away. She left the bed a tangle, hastily collecting clothes and shoes. Today she'd shower and dress in the master bath downstairs. In her current state, an encounter with Jack was the most dangerous risk she could imagine.

His door stood wide open, but she vowed to keep her eyes averted as she passed by. It didn't work. Some hostile polar force halted her dead in her tracks and compelled her to look inside his room.

"Oh, Lord," she moaned, transfixed by the sight of his bare backside. "Why me?"

Jack heard the gasp followed by her muffled entreaty, and felt a strong surge of satisfaction. Okay, so he wasn't playing fair. Neither was she. He'd tried to restrain himself. He really had. Last night, when the urge to kiss her overwhelmed him, he'd still kept the brakes on. Much as he'd wanted to, he hadn't grabbed her, devoured her mouth, or clamped her body so tightly against his, she wouldn't need to ask why he'd kissed her. It would have been patently clear.

He was furious that she hadn't taken the kiss seriously. What was so bloody damned difficult to understand? It seemed simple enough to him. She was a tempting woman; he was a man who desired her, in every way. Since she'd rebuffed his gentle overture, Jack didn't see that he had any choice other than to hit her with it, full force. That meant turning over right now and confronting her.

Temperance reasserted itself at the last second. He compromised. He did turn over and she did get an eyeful. But he feigned sleep. It took all his self-control to keep his eyes shut for the few tense seconds before he heard the *slap-slap* of her swiftly departing footsteps.

With an anguished groan, he rolled back over on his stomach. He hadn't anticipated that there would be this amount of physical suffering involved in a courtship.

After a few minutes' recovery time and a few more to shower, he struggled into some cutoffs and caught up with Kary in the kitchen. She had on a short white cotton jumpsuit with a bright red-and-yellow belt. Her wet braid was tied with a ribbon, and she was clutching her purse and a set of keys. "Going someplace?"

"Uh, yes." Her gaze flitted all over, refusing to land on him. "I have an appointment."

"At seven-fifteen?"

"Uh, yes," she repeated, crab-stepping her way to the door. "An early appointment."

"At seven-fifteen?"

She latched onto the knob. "At eight actually, but I don't want to be late."

"Unless it's in Houston, I don't think you have to worry." He opened the refrigerator. "Surely you have time for a bite before you take off. You're the one who used to sermonize about the importance of breakfast."

"I'll grab something on the way."

"Uh-uh, no fast food. Remember all those empty calories." He withdrew a gallon jug of milk. "How about I fix you a bowl of granola cereal and some yogurt?"

She slammed down her small red leather bag on the table and marched militantly toward him, wrenching the door open wider. "Never mind. I can take care of myself." Out came a pint of strawberries and a carton of whipping cream.

He watched her jerky motions as she rinsed the fruit and spread it on a paper towel to dry. She looked pale and tense, which cause Jack a pang of regret. The last thing he wanted to do was upset her. He didn't see any way to avoid it. In fact, he was getting ready to up the ante. He moved close, leaning on the counter where she worked. "Do you know anything about dreams?"

The cream she was pouring into a glass bowl sloshed over the rim. She blotted it, then crammed a pair of beaters in a hand-held mixer. "What about them?"

"I just wondered if, hypothetically speaking, a guy has an erotic dream—really juicy stuff, mind you—about someone he's known for years, but never, you know, thought of her in *that* way . . ."

"What's the question?" she snapped, cranking the mixer up to maximum speed.

"Well, do you think it means he wants her now . . . in *that* way?"

Above the machine's whine, he could barely hear her reply. "You're asking the wrong party. I'm no expert on the subject."

"Me either, but from a commonsense angle, it seems logical, doesn't it? That he must want her . . . sexually? Why else would he have a dream like that?"

"I'm sure I don't know."

Jack reached across, just inches from her breasts, and stole the plumpest berry. After outlining her lips with it, he bit it in two and tucked the other half into her mouth. Eyes locked, they both chewed, swallowed, and licked their lips. He now understood the true meaning of "weak in the knees." Other parts of him didn't feel weak at all.

"So what do you think?" he asked, his voice dense with hunger.

Her dark lashes weren't the longest he'd ever seen, but they were the thickest, and they curled naturally. "About what?"

"About those kinds of dreams."

"I think—oh, damn!" she exclaimed, horrified. "Look what you've made me do." Glaring at him, she pulled the plug. "I've whipped this cream into butter." She pawed through the cabinet above her, pulled out a jar of honey, and chucked a generous amount into the bowl. "Now I'll have to stir up a batch of biscuits to salvage this mess." Her eyes were wide; she sucked in her bottom lip. "I hate failure!"

For a second Jack was afraid she might cry. He realized that not once had he seen Karolyn Lucas shed a tear. He couldn't believe she'd dissolve now because her whipped cream hadn't turned out the way she'd planned. And then it hit him. She was used to succeeding so spectacularly that she had never learned to tolerate failure in any form. Maybe being a brilliant achiever wasn't such a great advantage after all.

Without stopping to think, he pulled her into his arms and held her fast. She smelled so good, like soft, sweet woman, not perfume. "Kary, try not to view this as a grand-scale screw-up, okay? We didn't need the whipped cream. The strawberries will taste better without it."

Her shoulders bucked. "No, they won't. You're just trying to placate me. Don't deny it."

Her breath when she spoke ruffled the hair on his chest. He shuddered. God, he wanted to touch her all over, and keep doing it all day. Instead he drew back far enough to tip up her chin and look her in the eyes. "Is it so improbable, my wanting to console you?"

She gave that some thought before saying solemnly, "For me, I think it would be very risky indeed if I were to accept comfort from you."

Jack was at a loss for words. Did she honestly see him as capable of hurting her? If anything, the opposite was true. She was going to belong to him. It would be his right and duty to take care of her, protect her. A sinking fear settled in his stomach. Kary showed every sign of needing strong persuasion. Suppose he didn't have what it took?

Nope, he couldn't buy that. He was too sure about the rightness of their being together. And he was going to start convincing her right now by kissing her the way he should have last night.

His hands framed her face. His lips descended to claim hers. She closed her eyes and so did he.

The doorbell rang.

They both jumped at the intrusion, staring at each other in disbelief. He let fly with a few choice words. She laughed a little nervously and quipped, "Saved by the bell."

"Who the devil's come calling at this time of day on Saturday?"

"Stay here. I'll go check."

Frustrated, Jack scowled as the door to the dining room swung shut behind her. He hadn't changed positions when she returned less than a minute later with a box in her hand and a dazed expression on her face. "Problem?"

She held up the package from a private messenger service. "The card says from my Secret Admirer, but there's no return address. What on earth can it be?"

He propped one shoulder against the refrigerator and crossed his arms. "Why not just open it and find out?"

"I'm almost afraid to," she whispered, stepping aside after she placed the box on the table.

Her hands shook so that he could tell the fear was real. "Come on, Kary, I'm sure it's not a bomb or anything." When she didn't move, he said, "Want me to do it for you?"

"No! I'll handle it myself." She sprang forward and reclaimed the square pack. "Why don't you go ahead and eat your breakfast?"

"And miss out on the unveiling? No way. Come on, rip 'er open."

She threw him a quelling glance, then set about the task, albeit in slow motion. *Hurry up, I can't stand the suspense.* His silent prodding did nothing to speed the process along. Just when he was about to pounce and tear the whole pile to shreds, she peeled the last bit of tape from the foil-wrapped inner present.

"Oh!" she breathed, raising both hands to cover her mouth while she stared at the intricate design of the Russian lacquer box. "Oh, I can't believe this."

Jack came closer, his eyes on her rather than the gift. "You like it?"

"It's magnificent." She touched the box reverently with her fingertips. "I've admired these for a long time, especially ones like this with so much detail, but . . ."

"You'd never buy it for yourself?" he guessed.

"No. They're far too expensive and too indulgent."

"Your mystery man obviously thinks you deserve to be indulged, with only the best."

As she gazed up at him he could see a shifting range of emotions reflected in her bright, intelligent eyes—astonishment, wariness, doubt, and panic.

"This is so unexpected, so inexplicable. I don't know *what* to think."

He lifted off the lid. "You missed something in here."

She peered inside and her already-pale face lost what color it had. She sagged into the nearest chair and rested her forehead on her palm. "Good Lord, Jack. This is too weird."

"I don't see what's so strange about—"

"Cashew nuts. I'm positively obsessed with them. How could he know that?"

Striving for nonchalance, he said, "Guess you have to give the guy points for being perceptive. He sure seems to understand exactly what it takes to impress you."

"That he does."

He was sure he caught a glimpse of exhilaration join the parade of other emotions. Good. His best-laid plans were finally starting to come together.

At six that evening, Karolyn tried the back-door and found it unlocked. Once again, she had hoped Jack might be otherwise occupied. No such luck. They were now into the second week of his visit and he had turned into a veritable homebody.

He had done yard work on Friday, so she hadn't had to get up and face the usual routine this morning. During the prior week, without being asked, he'd caught up on the countless small repairs and home-maintenance chores that she never had time for, and that Clint simply refused to do. He'd even found a match for the missing gingerbread trim on one of the upstairs gallery arches. At times he really was quite handy to have around.

But at other times, like this morning, she'd happily have beamed him up to Mars. She was a scientist, schooled in every facet and function of human anatomy, had dissected it down to its simplest form. So the sight of Jack sprawled amid rumpled sheets in all his naked, aroused glory shouldn't have inflamed her senses to the point of overload or driven her to envision the unthinkable.

Then to compound the torment, he'd hit her with that talk of erotic dreams. It was almost as if he'd gotten inside her head and asked the very questions that were plaguing her. It had taken her nearly all day to recoup, and still, at odd moments, aftershocks reverberated from that sudden blaze of explosive heat and insatiable hunger.

She put down her shopping bags and out of habit inserted her key into the deadbolt lock. The lacquer box and its bounty served as a centerpiece on the breakfast table, reminding her that she was besieged on two fronts. Jack and his earthy, in-your-face masculinity contrasted with the ethereal, romantic temptation of her secret admirer.

Karolyn didn't possess the feminine wiles to manage either of them. This was totally alien territory to her. She felt light-headed.

Jack elbowed through the swinging door, a can of beer in one hand, a stack of local tourist information in the other. "What have you done to yourself?"

She laughed, feeling even more light-headed because for once she had caught him off guard. "Something I've been contemplating for months." She fluffed her wispy new bangs and traced the sleek hairline over one ear to where it feathered along her neck. "I can't remember the last time I had short hair."

"I don't ever remember it. You've always worn a braid or two in some form." Depositing his beer and literature on the counter, he moved to examine her up close. He was very thorough, taking in not only the sassy, slightly tousled haircut, but the make-over of her face and the glossy watermelon-colored nail polish. "You've been busy today, Ms. Lucas."

She and Pepper had spent hours getting "the works" and the rest of the time trying on clothes and shoes. "Yes, well, sometimes it's nice to waste a day being frivolous."

He reached for the can and swallowed a long draft without taking his eyes off her. "Kary, I'm here to tell you, it was no waste. You look . . . ravishing."

Karolyn warned herself that it was silly and naive to bask in the glow of his compliment. Nor did she think it wise to thank him for it. But she couldn't control the liquid excitement that flowed through her any more than she could control the blush that tinted her cheekbones.

"Very pretty," he said, causing the blush to deepen.

When she couldn't bear his scrutiny any longer, she broke away and gathered up her booty from today's boutique blitz. It was then that she noticed the charcoal slacks and starched white-and-burgundy windowpane shirt he wore. His black leather belt with a signature buckle and matching loafers were the soft, expensive kind. He looked better than ravishing, but she'd keep that fact to herself. "Are you going out?"

"With any luck."

Unwelcome resentment boiled up inside her. "Dates have always come so easily for you, haven't they? Even at the last minute."

"Let's hope my victory string continues."

"Not to worry. I'm sure your record will hold." She couldn't get away fast enough.

He was faster, cutting her off before she could scuttle through the door. "That depends on you."

She looked down to where his fingers spanned her upper arm. No matter where, when, or how he touched her, her heartbeat shifted into high gear. "What do you want?"

"You. To go out with me."

"Me?" Intuition told her that what he had in mind was a thing apart from the casual meals they had shared up till now. "And you?"

He nodded.

She wanted to ask why, as she'd done last night, but didn't because she feared a similar answer. She wanted to refuse, but didn't because the lure of forbidden excitement overwhelmed reason. "Where?" she asked, dry-mouthed.

"Why don't you change into something that goes with your new look and I'll show instead of tell?"

Clutching the twine handles of her shopping bags, Karolyn drifted up to her room in a trance. She really had gone crazy. She'd tacitly agreed to a date—there was no other word for it—with a man who had forgotten more seduction techniques than she'd be able to learn in a lifetime.

And all she could think about was what to wear. Any doctor worthy of a caduceus would diagnose her as certifiably insane.

The remarkable thing was, she didn't care.

She hopped into the shower for a minute, then dried, powdered, and slathered herself with the lotion Clint had given her last Christmas. It had a lush yet elusive scent that before tonight had always struck her as a tad too obvious. Tonight she dabbed her pulse points with the companion perfume.

Then, without examining her motives too closely, she chose one of the impulse purchases she'd made that day. Airy as vapor, the gossamer pastel print georgette billowed over her head and skimmed down her body. The sheer fabric was transparent enough to be provocative, and just dense enough to escape being scandalous.

Pepper had assured her this was the latest fashion rage. Karolyn took her word for it. Pepper kept tabs on such things. Low-heeled sandals the color of French vanilla ice cream and a tiny natural straw shoulder bag completed the outfit. Wearing this dress, and the barest of essentials under it, made her feel light and free, as if she were floating on a cloud.

Jack stood waiting for her at the foot of the staircase, as if she were a debutante and he her awestruck escort. He didn't say anything, but the glint in his eyes and the lazy half smile signaled approval loud and clear. His mouth opened, revealing just the tip of his tongue, then a second's flash of teeth.

Karolyn's body answered the ageless invitation, tautening from a wild craving that made her want to jump on him, wrestle him down to her mother's Tabriz prayer rug, and order that mouth to do wicked, wicked things to her.

"Don't tempt me," he said, and again he seemed to be reading her thoughts.

It was going to be a long evening, but she wanted to relish every moment of it. Never before had she felt so daring, so unfettered, and tonight might be the chance of a lifetime to make the most of it. Like Cinderella, tomorrow she'd go back to being a drudge. "I'm ready for you to show me."

All he said was, "Oh, Kary," but his voice was heavily laden with promise.

As he guided her toward where he'd parked on the street, his hand at the back of her waist seared like a branding iron. How odd that her skin had recently become hypersensitive. "The top's down."

He opened the passenger door of his rakish Mustang convertible. It had never occurred to

Karolyn that you could rent something so sporty, but of course Jack would be an expert in this area. "I'll put it back up if you don't want to ruin your new hairdo."

"No, leave it down." Zipping along in a convertible enhanced the illusion of freedom. "That's supposed to be one of the benefits of this windblown look. You just rearrange it with your fingers."

"Okay, you're the boss."

"Yes." Karolyn relaxed in her bucket seat, suddenly feeling very much in charge. That was probably an illusion, too, like everything else about tonight, but she'd already made the choice to abandon herself to it for the duration.

The sun had dropped behind a large bank of fleecy clouds on the horizon, and balmy tropical air, fresh with the sea's tang, swirled all around, playing with her hair and the soft fabric of her dress. Several times she exchanged smiles with Jack as he drove, but neither was anxious to talk. She was too busy storing up every small detail.

All too quickly he pulled into a parking lot on the Strand. "This is one of the parts I like most about Galveston. You can get almost anywhere you want to go in ten minutes."

"I suppose lots of people would say that's because there aren't many places to go."

"More than enough to satisfy me." He came around the car, and when she gave him her hand to be helped out, he kept holding it while they crossed the uneven brick street and entered the restaurant.

Karolyn had eaten at the Wentletrap a number of times over the past three years. This evening the Victorian bar, three-story atrium, and brick archways took on the aura of a marvelously intimate setting, the perfect backdrop for romance. "This is one of my favorite places," she confessed shortly after they were seated.

"Then I'm sure it'll be one of mine too."

She returned his smile with one of her own—couldn't help herself. So this was how it worked, she mused. The notorious Rowland technique. When Jack applied himself, he really could be disgracefully charming and courtly. The only misgiving she had at the moment was why he'd opted to practice it on her. Then she chided herself for the negative thought. Tomorrow would be soon enough to start questioning. "Did you pick here because it was mentioned in one of your tourist guides?"

He seemed engrossed in the wine list. "No, I've been out and about a little bit over the last week. Talked to some people. Several recommended this as the best spot for a, um, good meal."

He also seemed evasive. "I don't think you'll be disappointed."

"I don't think so either." In the dim glow of candlelight, his blue eyes appeared darker than usual, and very, very intense. "In fact, I'm sure of it."

The only thing Karolyn could be sure of was that she was already in too deep.

They agreed on wine, tasted and approved it, then took several sips in silence. Although she didn't want to raise the intrusive subject of Tammy, she was too curious to avoid it. "Last night, out on the porch, were you referring to this when you said we had plans?"

"Nah, I made that up on the spot. In case you didn't get the message, I'll spell it out plainly. I am not interested in stirring up something with Tammy. She was a twit back in high school and I can't see any outward signs of improvement."

His insight filled her with a savage burst of satisfaction. "So this"—she made a gesture that encompassed the potted palms, white-painted cast-iron columns, and well-dressed crowd—"is a spur-of-the-moment idea?"

"More like contingency plan B. Originally I

had in mind to ask you to run up to Houston with me today."

A ripple of anxiety tightened her chest. "Tired of Galveston already?" she asked lightly.

"Hardly. I wanted you along so we could drive the rental car back to the airport after picking up my new one."

"You're buying a car? Why?"

"It's a Jeep Cherokee—actually more like a station wagon—and I'm buying it because I'll need transportation."

"But isn't that a waste when you're out of the country for a good percentage of the time? Clint says it makes more sense just to rent for the short time he needs one."

He set down his wineglass a little too deliberately, she noticed. "Kary, what's it going to take to convince you I'm through globe-trotting? I told you I'm back to settle down and I mean to go the whole route."

"The whole route?"

"Yep. That's why I decided on the Jeep. It'll make a solid, dependable vehicle for a family, baby seats and all."

FIVE

Karolyn clung to her wineglass with a desperate grip while her addled brain sifted through all the data. It finally homed in on the nucleus of what he'd said. "Baby seats?"

"Well, yeah. Isn't that the order of things? You make up your mind to settle down, and before you know it, there are a couple of baby seats in the back of your car and you're sweating the cost of college educations."

All she could think about was Jack making babies with some anonymous woman. She blinked furiously when the menu she'd just been presented blurred before her eyes. During stressful times, she had to restrain herself from popping out the contacts and stomping on them. So much for self-improvement. "There are always scholarships."

"Tons of them for wizards like you who make

perfect scores on their SATs." He lifted both shoulders. "But for me to produce kids with enough smarts to qualify, I'd have to mix genes with a super-intelligent mate and hope for the best. Isn't that the way genetics works?"

"Not necessarily. Offspring of intellectually superior people tend to deviate toward the norm." Brilliant, Karolyn, reciting straight from a first-year-psych textbook.

"That's only half-true in your family. Clint's reasonably sharp, but probably not up there on the same plane as your parents with their doctorates in biochemistry." He tipped his glass to her. "You, on the other hand, blow the norm theory all to hell. How do you account for that deviation?"

She couldn't. Besides, this discussion of genetically engineered children was putting a damper on her fantasy. "I'm going to have the seared salmon with fresh pineapple salsa," she said briskly, decisively. "And as a side order, no more talk about IQs."

He laughed and picked up his menu. "Yes, ma'am. Even an average guy like yours truly is quick enough to see it's a sore point."

"How would you like being constantly judged by a single criterion? All people ever say is 'Oh, that's Karolyn Lucas. She's so smart it's freaky.'

Like I belong in a carnival sideshow. They think because I always made all A's in all subjects that I must not be normal, that my head is full of nothing but complex, esoteric theories and research findings. But most irritating is their assumption that I can't possibly want the same things in life as everyone else." She banged the table twice with her fist. "Just once I'd like somebody to look at me and see more than a collection of gray matter."

In the heartbeat it took Jack to unclench her fingers and cover them with his, Karolyn was already regretting the lengthy temperamental tirade. She had meant to keep things breezy and upbeat, the proper tone, she imagined, for this sort of situation. In contrast to how easily she learned most things, social graces had always been tricky for her to master.

He leaned close, his hand still pinning hers. "I'm looking at you right now, and what I see is a gorgeous woman. Your eyes sparkle, like maybe you're keeping some very intriguing secrets. You have smooth skin, soft and tempting to touch, a saucy little tipped-up nose, a sweet mouth, and perfect dainty ears that invite a man to whisper his own secrets."

Karolyn barely managed to swallow her wine without spraying it all over him. It wasn't that he was looking at her. It was the *way* he was doing it . . . as if he might really be seeing the woman he'd described. No, the possibility was too absurd. "I don't need your gratuitous compliments," she said pugnaciously.

She saw a flicker of hurt in his eyes before impatience replaced it. "Is it too much to expect a 'Thank you, Jack' when I've paid you *sincere* compliments? Barring that, a demure blush would be acceptable."

"You have me confused with all your other women."

His hand shifted so his thumb could stroke the tops of her fingers. "Believe me, Kary, I would never confuse you with anyone else, because you're different from every other woman I've known."

"Right. I guess that leads us full circle, doesn't it? Back to how different I am."

His thumb stilled. "You're in an unusually combative mood all of a sudden. Care to tell me why?"

Why not? All this tooing and froing was making her so tense she couldn't stop fidgeting. "Okay, you asked for it. I don't like to play games when I don't know the rules." She slid her hand free of his and pointed her index finger at him.

"You, Jack Rowland, are playing some kind of game with me."

"What makes you think so?"

"You've turned sweet and nice, which is totally out of character. Instead of heckling me, you've bent over backward to be considerate and charming. It drives me batty that I can't figure out what you're up to. You didn't even make fun of my gift from the secret admirer."

"Maybe I thought it would be rude to belittle something you plainly liked a lot."

"Since when did rudeness ever stop you?" She shook her head in disbelief. "Then there's tonight. You're treating me like a real date, all company manners and syrupy compliments. Who wouldn't be suspicious?"

"You know, Kary, I'm beginning to wonder if you're half as smart as you're supposed to be. In certain areas, you can be amazingly dim-witted."

"Why you—" she cut herself off, chuckling when she realized she'd fallen into her own trap. How could she take offense at his remark when only moments ago she'd practically begged to have her brains discredited? "Touché. Now, something tells me we'll get along much more amicably if we change the subject. Agreed?"

Without moving, he caught the waiter's eye from across the room, another useful talent she'd never perfected. "Agreed. But first let me remind you of an old Texas saying."

"Which one?"

"I may tell you the truth four or five different ways, but I'll never lie to you. If you remember that and listen to what I say, it'll all come clear."

His cryptic advice aside, Karolyn had a splendid time for the remainder of the evening. After dinner they attended an outdoor concert on the grounds of Ashton Villa, a restored Victorian mansion. Then Jack suggested they go back to a club in the historic district and listen to jazz. In place of a nightcap they took a hand-in-hand stroll along the beach and got so wrapped up in their conversation, they wound up walking all the way to the twenty-four-hour fishing pier at Ninetieth and Seawall.

It was past one when they made it back to the car. Karolyn was relaxed and mellow. If she forgot the past and didn't worry about the future, Jack was an ideal companion. He encouraged her to laugh, twirl barefoot in the sand, and even test her flirting skills a little. Heady stuff.

The only disappointment came when they got back to the house. Jack left her at the door, saying he wanted to walk around the neighborhood for a while before calling it a night.

She wanted him to kiss her.

❈──────────────❈

Karolyn woke early and rolled out of bed, energized even though she'd slept only a few hours. She must still be riding the residual high from her dream date. "Don't get carried away, Lucas," she admonished herself. "Time for a reality check."

She showered, marveling at how little time it took to dry and style her new haircut. If she'd known how easy and carefree it would be, she'd have had it cut long ago.

Pancakes. She had a craving for them. Jack would be sleeping in, she was sure, because although she'd read for an hour after going to bed, she hadn't heard him return. Feeling generous, she decided to make a big batch so he could heat some up when he woke.

She stared resolutely at the floor and tiptoed noiselessly past his door and down the stairs. He was already in the kitchen, the Sunday edition of the *Galveston Daily News* spread out on the table. His eyes were bloodshot and heavy-lidded, as if he hadn't slept at all.

"Morning, Kary."

His voice sounded low, gritty. It set her nerve endings to humming like live wires. She pulled the sash on her eggplant-colored cotton robe tighter and bustled over to the cabinets. "How do buttermilk pancakes sound?"

"I'm easy. Whatever you're in the mood for is fine with me."

Karolyn's fingers froze on the mixing bowl. Was he suggesting . . . ? Think reality, she reminded herself. Except reality was the fact that she and Jack were playing house. With her assuming the lion's share of the cooking and him being Mr. Fix-it, they'd been acting out the traditional parts of a married couple, circa 1950.

No, that picture wasn't quite right either. There was one facet of their peculiar relationship that didn't resemble a marriage at all. They weren't sharing a bed.

But if, as Jack insisted, he was going to put down roots and start a family, he'd soon be hunting a woman to fill that role. Her hand turned so clammy on the knob, it took several tries before she got the pantry door open.

While the griddle heated she whisked together flour, eggs, oil, and milk. When a drop of water she flicked on the griddle sizzled, she carefully measured out the proper amount of batter.

"Where do you stand on this condom business?"

The hand she was pouring the second cake

with took a wild swing. The pancake ended up in the shape of Florida. "Condoms?"

"You know, the school district is going to give them out at Ball High. Part of a program to—"

"I know why they're giving them out." Heedless of etiquette, she tossed some silverware and napkins on the table, then carried over pitchers of melted butter and syrup.

He lowered the paper and the lines around his eyes seemed more pronounced. From fatigue? Laughter? "I'm sure you do."

She had no idea how to interpret that. "The teenage pregnancy rate here is staggering. I think district officials are desperate to try anything to curb it."

"Do you agree this is the way to do it, though? For instance, if it was your daughter, would you want her getting contraceptives at school?"

She flipped a short stack on a plate, poured a fresh batch, and slapped his down in front of him. No hash-house fry cook could have done better. "If it were my daughter, I would hope we had covered the subject in sufficient depth that the school needn't be involved."

"Did your mother handle the birds and bees that way?"

She turned back to the stove to flip her pancakes. Why did their mealtime talk tend to veer off on such bizarre tangents? "Mom, as you might guess, took the scientific approach. Lots of anatomical charts, schematic drawings, and working models, so yes, I had a thorough understanding of human reproductive systems at an early age."

"It's a good idea to learn all the technicalities, I guess." She sat down across from him and he paused in his attack on the food. "But to most teenagers that textbook stuff is just so many words once their hormones go on a rampage. The old biological urge to, uh, mate is often a lot more powerful than a person's will to resist."

The heavy cadence of Karolyn's heartbeat pounded in her throat. "Therein lies the problem," she said shakily. She was finding out fast how all-consuming the hunger could be. Being a late-bloomer hadn't blunted the potency of it. "But you have to control it."

"Funny, that's what my dad always preached to me. 'Jack, that's the true measure of being a man. You have to learn to control yourself where the ladies are concerned.'"

"Given your aversion to obedience, I'm sure you did your best to ignore his advice."

He pushed aside his plate and directed the full force of his gaze on her. "Let's spread this out on the table right now, Kary. Regardless of what you seem to think about my prowess or proclivities, I have always, always behaved responsibly toward women."

Until now. Now you're trifling with me unmercifully, whether you mean to or not.

"In short, I have no reason to look over my shoulder about anything that happened in the past." Lack of sleep did nothing to diminish the spellbinding impact of his eyes. "Nor will there be any unpleasant surprises in the future." He scooted his chair back and stood. "Is that clear enough for you to comprehend, or do I need to get more graphic with the details?"

The first bite of pancakes turned to chaff in her mouth. She had to drink a whole glass of raspberry-banana juice to wash it down. Her appetite vanished. Jack's nearness, his ease in talking about an act as elemental as mating, even his scratchy voice and beard stubble were so compelling she wanted to disregard caution and logic and consequences—untie her robe and see how responsibly he behaved toward her, how well he controlled his urges.

Common sense prevailed. She stood, too, and scooped up her plate. "These pancakes taste doughy. I must have made a mistake when I measured." She fed them to the disposal while he cleared the table. As the grinding noise wound down she heard the front doorbell ringing. Karolyn welcomed the interruption and rushed to see who was out so early on Sunday morning.

She opened the door and her stomach went into free-fall. This gambit got more outlandish by the day. A uniformed woman extended a tiny package and said, "I have a delivery for Karolyn Lucas." With a shaky hand, Karolyn scribbled her signature on the clipboard.

"What now?"

Jack's voice startled her. She whirled around, bobbling the package she'd been weighing in her palm. He snagged it in midair and eyed it disdainfully. "Card's missing, but I guess it's no big mystery as to who sent this. It's about the size of a ring box from a jewelry store." Smirking, he said, "Wow, Kary, do you think he's asking you to get engaged?"

"No, I do not!" she snapped, more than a little relieved that he'd reverted to his cantankerous ways. She felt much more capable of dealing with him on those terms.

She seized her latest surprise from his grasp and tore off the small square of wrapping paper. Nestled inside the velvet-lined rose-quartz box was a thimble made of bone china and edged in gold. Painted on the side with the finest of brush strokes were the entwined figures of Romeo and

Juliet. Karolyn couldn't speak and couldn't stop shaking her head.

"You look like you've seen a ghost. What's the big deal about a thimble?"

"I've been collecting them for years," she murmured. "At last count I had close to two hundred. They're packed away now because there wasn't any place to display them when I moved back here." Karolyn dropped like dead-weight onto an Italian giltwood stool. "But how did *he* know?"

"You wanna figure out who this character is, Kary?"

She nodded, "Oh, yes." If she could solve that riddle, maybe she could restore some semblance of order to her life.

"Then here's your clue." He speared his little finger into the thimble and waved it back and forth before her. "The first step is to make a list of every man who knows about your hobby."

A stirring of female pride prevented her from blurting out that she had always kept the collection in her bedroom, and that no man had ever been there to see it. "It could be any one of a number of people," she said, dissembling.

"Okay, use that list and mark those who are also aware of your cashew fetish. One of them has to be Santa Claus and his bag of toys. I'd have thought you would come up with this on your own. It's a matter of simple logic."

Simple, perhaps, assuming one were capable of logical thought. That had been in short supply since Jack appeared on the scene. As for the secret admirer, that defied any attempt at logic. "I'll have to work on it later."

Karolyn made tracks up the stairs. She had planned to go to church anyway; might as well make it the early service.

She had never needed divine guidance more urgently.

Karolyn held her half of the hymnal and sang "Love Lifted Me" by rote while her mind wandered. The familiar rituals weren't having the desired effect, primarily because the source of her problem was standing close enough to hold the other half of the songbook.

Jack was harder to shake than a summer cold. Who'd have thought he could shower, shave, dress in a coat and tie, and be waiting for her by the time she was ready? Ubiquitous, that was the word for him. He'd just moved in and invaded every corner of her existence.

As the closing organ notes faded away the minister said, "Let us pray." Karolyn bowed her head, and still, her thoughts strayed. She hadn't even had much opportunity to examine and evaluate her feelings about her enigmatic secret admirer.

Whether she was awake or sleeping, Jack demanded too much of her attention. Telling herself to pull back was useless—he had no concept of what keeping a reasonable distance meant. Everywhere she turned, he was just *there*.

Damn Clint for setting her up this way. Oh, dear. It was hard to think charitably toward her brother, but this was the last place she should be damning him. She squinched her eyes more tightly and forced herself to pay heed to Dr. Harvey's words. They focused, ironically enough, on what it means to truly love our fellowman.

Damn! There really was no haven.

Jack raised his head after the benediction and smiled at Kary. She looked flustered, as he must have at fourteen when his mother walked into his bedroom and caught him in the middle of a wild adolescent fantasy involving a *Playboy* centerfold. He suspected Kary's fantasies ran along tamer lines, but would have paid big bucks to read her mind and find out for sure.

They exchanged greetings with the minister

and several members of the congregation who recognized Jack and came up to welcome him back. He was pretty sure more than one elderly lady beamed with satisfaction at seeing him there with Kary. Probably thought she'd be a positive influence on him. In a way, they were justified in thinking so. He had reformed because of Kary.

"Ready to go?" he asked, impatient to leave the crowd. He cupped her elbow and gallantly steered her toward the parking lot. She looked classy and feminine in her red silk dress. The pleated skirt rippled interestingly when she walked and the white-trimmed belt emphasized her small waist. He even liked the wide-brimmed white hat.

"Were you surprised to see so many of the same people still going to the same church?"

"Not surprised exactly. More like reassured. The sense of continuity appeals to me. It's the right sort of atmosphere for bringing up a family."

She got the same stricken look she'd worn last night when he had mentioned baby seats. "Are you sure the pod people didn't sneak in and take over your body while you were sleeping? All this talk about stability and roots sounds decidedly alien to me."

"How often am I going to have to remind you

that I've changed." He unlocked her door, and before she could gather the skirt in, he solicitously did it for her. He took his time smoothing it along her thigh, wondering if she had any idea how obsessed he was becoming with her legs, that he'd mortgage his soul to touch them.

She watched his hand move in slow motion past her knee, then her eyes, dancing with mirth, met his. "Looks like the same old Jack to me."

Yep, she knew. He flashed her a grin, but didn't bother trying to make it apologetic. "Okay, so there are a few remnants of my former self hanging on."

"As I have to keep reminding *you*, some things never change."

Undaunted, he jumped in the car, whipped it around, and headed for Sixty-first. Kary would never believe he could get excited about something so mundane as going to church, eating Sunday dinner at a cafeteria, and then spending the rest of the day relaxing with her. Granted, most of his excitement probably stemmed from what he intended to show her after they ate.

At least three times during their meal he almost spilled the beans. Keeping secrets was still new to him.

"Where are we off to now?" she asked when he bypassed the turn for P ½.

"The East End Historical District."

"Going to give me a tour?" She sounded amused by the possibility.

"You could say that." He pulled up in front of a Victorian on Postoffice Street and parked in the shady overhang of a large live-oak tree. A realtor's sign sporting a "Sold" banner was planted close to the curb between two bushy oleanders.

"Somebody's already bought this house and I didn't even know it was for sale," Kary said. "I always thought it was a shame that it stood vacant for so long. These old beauties need people who care about them living inside. Otherwise they show signs of neglect very quickly."

Knowing that Kary had spent most of her life in a house very much like this one had influenced Jack's decision. He was banking on familiarity and sentiment working in his favor. "It was completed in 1887."

"That's the same year my parents' home was built." She got out and studied the facade. "This one is a little bigger and fancier, but there are lots of similarities, like the rounded arches, double galleries, and fish-scale shingles."

He came around and grabbed her hand, eagerly tugging her forward. "This is one of the best things about the whole place. See this *R* on the front gate? That's the original owner's initial. It's inscribed in the sidewalk too."

The ornate iron fence and gate was less than waist-high due to grade raising after the 1900 hurricane. He bent to trip the latch and with a flourish gestured her inside. "Look," he said, pointing with his toe. "It says JRR."

"Are you suggesting there's some cosmic significance here because your first and last initials are the same?"

"Well, no, but you have to admit it's an interesting coincidence."

"I'll buy that."

Jack produced the key from his pants pocket and led her up the ten steps to the beveled-glass front doors. "Wait till you see the inside. It needs a little work, but it's got great potential."

She stepped through the double doors into the mosaic-tiled entry. Just as his had the first time, her gaze went immediately to the coffered mahogany ceiling. "Very nice," she said reverently. "Beautiful detail."

She was already hooked. He could tell by the appreciative gleam in her eyes. And as he drew her into each successive room, it grew brighter. They started up the stairs, but she paused on the first landing. "The colors in this oleander design on the stained-glass window are wonderful." She examined it for a long time before continuing to the second floor.

"The unusual thing about this house is that it's stayed in the same family for most of the past hundred years," Jack told her. "When the last descendant died, the estate got tied up in a probate battle and that's why nobody's lived here recently."

"I guess that explains why so many of the original fixtures and ornamentation are still in place, and why it didn't get cut up into apartments and eventually gutted."

"Yeah, the agent said the door locks, window latches, even the curtain rods are original. The kitchen needs updating, but everything else is basically cosmetic. It'll just take some time and effort."

They went into a front corner room where narrow slats of sunlight penetrated the floor-to-ceiling shutters. Jack folded them back to reveal a pair of walk-out windows that led into the upstairs gallery. "Another touch of home," she mused, "though the tree is missing."

"Kind of a shame, really. I have fond memories of all those nights Clint and I sneaked out."

They walked through the other three rooms, then climbed a flight of narrower steps to the single large open area on the third floor. "This could be finished and used for a rec room, like we have. Just don't try coaxing a pool table up those stairs."

Jack took a deep breath and said, "I had in mind converting it to a playroom, with built-in bookshelves, closets, and hinged toy chests."

The silence was deafening. He saw her swallow, then suck in her bottom lip. "We're not here just out of curiosity, are we?"

"No."

"That 'Sold' sign out front is yours?"

"Yes."

"Oh, Jack, you shouldn't have made such an important decision this fast. I know you think you want to stay here for good, but what if that turns out to be a passing fancy? You've plunked down a considerable amount of money for something that may end up being an albatross."

"I will be living here for a long time, Kary," he said firmly. "I want my children to grow up in this house."

"I see." She crossed her arms in front of her. The movement created a hint of cleavage. Jack started sweating more than normal. He had left his tie and jacket in the backseat, but the power in the house hadn't been switched on yet and the air was stifling. "What do you plan to do about a job?

There can't be much demand in Galveston for the kind of engineering you do."

"Fortunately I don't have to worry about that right away. Over the past dozen years I've made a sizable chunk of money. Since there wasn't much to spend it on, I invested the lion's share, and those investments have turned out to be profitable ones. I'm more than able to support a family."

"I guess you're old enough, and presumably smart enough, to know what you're doing without advice from me." She stuck out her chin, threw back her shoulders, and made a beeline for the steps.

He couldn't believe how fast she got to the bottom in her heels. She as halfway out the front door before he could stop her. "Wait! There's something I want you to see in the backyard." Jack knew he sounded like a kid boasting about his Christmas toys. What the hell. He had a right to be proud of this one.

She stood still for a long time before turning around. When she did, the corners of her mouth tipped up in a strained imitation of her real smile. "As long as I'm here, why not get the complete tour, right?"

"Right." They went out the backdoor and down more steps to the yard. Weeds had invaded the St. Augustine grass and choked the flower beds. Another project. But there was one anomaly, a bright spot. Near the back fence was a white arbor with pink and yellow roses climbing up the sides and over the top. Inside were two benches shaded by the rampant growth of the rose canes. He led her there and took the seat facing her.

"So, what do you think?"

"About the house?"

"Uh-huh."

She removed her hat, traced the edge of the brim with one finger, then lay it on her lap. "Honestly?"

"Uh-huh."

"I wish it were mine."

Her wistful confession hit him like a gut shot. It was all he could do to keep from revealing everything. Somehow he managed to keep a lid on it. "Really? You have some ideas for what you'd do to bring it up to snuff?"

Her only reply was a silent nod.

"That's good. I can use expert advice." He was talking fast, doing a hard sell. "I want the end product to have the same feel as your family's home. I'm assuming you must have inherited your mother's taste and style. Who better to act as my consultant for the renovation?"

"You want me to . . . to . . . oh, never

mind!" She mangled the hat brim while he watched her struggle to organize her thoughts. "Jack, let me give you a crash course in sensitivity training. You do not ask one woman to decorate another's house. Not even if one is a professional."

"How come?"

She blew out an exasperated breath. "We're dealing with a subtlety that eludes the male brain. Trust me when I tell you that if I do this house, your future wife will be sure to want major changes, and probably at great expense."

"I want you to do it, Kary."

Her hat slipped to the ground. "Why are you being so perverse?"

"Because I know what I want." And what he wanted was her lips. Right now. He could see nothing beyond them, and she knew it.

"No, Jack," she said breathlessly. "I don't think you ought to do what you're thinking about doing."

He leaned forward while she was speaking, close enough to feel her breath. "I'm through thinking about it. And this time I'm going to do it right."

SIX

The rational side of Karolyn's brain told her to pull back or, wiser still, to run. But she'd grown so tired of thinking analytically. With Jack, it was almost instinctive to let her emotions take over. That part of her eagerly, shamelessly craved the kiss.

"Look at me, Kary."

She hadn't realized she'd closed her eyes, but when she opened them and gazed into the dark blue depths of his, the desire there was unmistakable. It fed her own.

This was what she had been wanting for days, what she had probably been wanting for much longer than that. "Jack."

"Yes." His hands framed her face, thumbs stroking at the corners of her mouth, urging her to open and accommodate him. When she did, a husky groan of satisfaction vibrated in his throat. And the magic began.

His tongue slipped between her lips, a gentle, coaxing seducer that quickly transformed into a bold, demanding conquerer. Probing, swirling, it touched off sensations so powerful, so wondrous, Karolyn felt as if she had never before been kissed. At least not by anyone who knew how to do it so thoroughly and so well.

Nor had she ever experienced such delicious intimacy as that created by the in-and-out, over-and-under dueling of their tongues. Her lips parted wider and she rested both hands on his shoulders, a silent appeal for him to deepen the kiss.

Without breaking the connection between them, he dropped to his knees and fitted his hands to her waist, drawing her closer. Heavy afternoon heat enveloped them, but it was nothing compared with the fire he ignited inside her. She arched her back, a spontaneous movement that molded her breasts to his chest.

Karolyn heard a faint, needy sound escape her lips and be quickly absorbed by the hungry insistence of his mouth. Palms cupping her shoulder blades, he rocked her against him, a steady, pulsating rhythm that was incredibly provocative, incredibly arousing. It evoked images of skin sliding over skin, whispered promises, and boundless pleasure.

She was so keenly attuned now . . . to the taste and scent of him, to the thrust and acceptance of his body. And to her own capacity for passion. She wanted to test the limits of this newly discovered facet of herself, to see how far it would take her. She wanted to get closer still.

Her legs shifted restlessly and suddenly he was kneeling between them, pressing her hard against him, giving her what she longed for. Soon, even that wasn't enough. She needed more than the clinging warmth of his lips and the solid reassurance of his strength. She needed proof that his passion matched her own, but short of being unspeakably daring, how did one confirm such a thing?

Jack dared. His hand seared a path from her ankle to her knee, and then, after a second's pause, his fingers skimmed along her inner thigh to touch the secret spot where she was most vulnerable . . . and most receptive.

"Ahhh, Jack!" she cried out, swept up on a wave of ecstasy. Her heart hammered, its savage beat echoing in every part of her body. She discovered what it meant to surrender to a man's embrace, to be possessed by his ravenous mouth and avid hands.

His breath was hot on her neck, his voice thick and raspy in her ear. "I want to make love with you, Kary. Now. Right here, surrounded by the roses."

Karolyn shuddered, and for a few tense seconds she flirted with the temptation to give in. Then reality struck like an icy wind. She could barely breathe; words were even more difficult. "Jack, surely you see that's impossible. I could never—"

Recoiling, she broke off, her throat suddenly tight and painful. Of course, she had to blame herself for allowing him the liberties in the first place, but his callousness astounded her. Making love here, now, would be an insult to both her and his future bride.

Anger banished the incipient tears. "Do you really think I'm stupid or gullible enough to get involved in anything so temporary and pointless?"

Jack swore softly. Grimacing, he withdrew and hiked himself back onto the opposite bench, resting low on his spine, knees spread wide. The proof of his desire that she'd been seeking moments ago was visible and considerable.

Because he didn't try to conceal it, Karolyn had trouble concentrating on anything else. She was mortified, yet at the same time fascinated, and so hot she was perilously close to melting. It wasn't fair that this one man could dominate her senses so easily and completely.

Brows drawn together, he appeared quite fierce and unyielding. "If only you'd look at what we both want from the right perspective, it makes perfect sense."

"Maybe that's the way it seems from *your* perspective. From mine, the consequences far outweigh a few fleeting . . . benefits."

"I promise there'd be more than a 'few' benefits and I would do my best to make sure they weren't fleeting." Through half-closed eyes, he stared at her mouth. "As for consequences, I can take care of them too."

Karolyn tipped her head back against the arbor. The sweet smell of roses did nothing to soothe her. Jack had kept her in almost constant turmoil over the past few days.

It would undoubtedly get a great deal worse—because her feelings for him were far more complicated than a case of sexual curiosity, or even lust. Karolyn could now concede she had nursed a childhood crush on Jack. She was very much afraid that it had matured into something precariously close to love. It was the most imprudent thing she could have done, yet how did one control such things? She had to try.

"I need only one promise from you."

"Ask."

"Swear this will never happen again." Her hands were shaky and so was her voice. "Swear it."

"No dice, Kary." He reached across and brought her hand to his heart; held it in place by covering it with his. His heart beat the same riotous cadence as hers. "The only promise I'm making is that the next time we start, we're going to finish. Keep that in mind."

Karolyn bent over her bike's handlebars and raced down Bernardo de Galvez Street. Like a fugitive being chased by a posse, she felt hunted. No place was safe, least of all her home. Not as long as Jack stayed there.

When Avenue P dead-ended at Seawall, she leaned into the turn without slowing down. At this hour on Monday morning the walks on both sides were deserted except for an occasional runner or roller blader. She could ride as fast and as recklessly as her legs could pedal.

Reckless. The last word she'd have applied to herself. Until yesterday. Now, given her shocking behavior in the backyard, it was the only term to describe her. No, better add dumb to the list too. It was reckless and dumb to lose control that way. But at the time she'd been under the spell of something more powerful than her own will.

Jack's words, the thrilling way he'd touched her, and the image of them together, doing what they'd both wanted, kept haunting her. A more tangible reminder was the lingering ache deep inside her.

She hadn't seen or spoken to him since their silent ride back to her parents' house, whereupon she'd holed up in her room until this morning. Avoiding Jack was the only way to guarantee there would be no repeat of yesterday afternoon's near miss. By owning up to her weakness, she could exercise caution.

Most mornings Karolyn took Seawall as far as Tenth Street before cutting up to the medical center. Today, without making a conscious decision, she veered onto Thirteenth and after several blocks turned on Postoffice. Telling herself she was a glutton for punishment, she braked in front of Jack's Victorian.

She couldn't believe he'd actually bought the first house he'd been shown, but that's what he claimed. Indeed, he seemed proud to have accomplished the task so quickly. Had she been shopping for a home, she would have wanted to look at everything available, then contemplate

WIN THE ROMANTIC VACATION OF A LIFETIME...
PLUS $5000 SPENDING MONEY!

Take your pick — Hawaii, Europe or the Caribbean — and enjoy 14 passion-filled days and sultry nights if you're the winner of the Winners Classic Sweepstakes presented by Loveswept. It's *free* to enter, so don't miss out!

YOU COULD WIN YOUR DREAM TRIP!

Just peel off the FREE ENTRY side of our bright red heart, and place it on the Entry Form to the right. But don't stop there!

...AND GET LOVESWEPT EVERY MONTH!

Use the FREE BOOKS sticker and you'll get your first shipment of 6 Loveswept Romance books absolutely free! PLUS, we'll sign you up for the most romantic book service in the world! About once a month you get 6 new Loveswept novels hot off the presses before they are available in bookstores. You'll always have 15 days to examine the books, and if you decide to keep them, YOU'LL SAVE OVER FIVE DOLLARS OFF bookstore prices with each shipment! What's more, there's NO CHARGE FOR SHIPPING AND HANDLING. So you can enjoy the convenience of home delivery at no extra cost. There's no minimum to buy. And you can cancel any time by writing "cancel" on your invoice and returning the books to us. We'll even pay the postage.

Get a FREE lighted makeup case and 6 free Loveswept books!

Open the tortoise-shell finish case and the mirror lights up! Comes with a choice of brushes for lips, eyes and cheek blusher.

BOTH GIFTS ARE YOURS TO KEEP NO MATTER WHAT!

DON'T HOLD BACK!

1. **No obligation!** No purchase necessary! Enter our Sweepstakes for a chance to win!
2. **FREE!** Get your first shipment of 6 Loveswept books FREE plus a lighted makeup case as a free gift.
3. **Save money!** Save OVER FIVE DOLLARS OFF bookstore prices with future shipments. Return any shipment you don't want.
4. Enjoy the convenience of FREE HOME DELIVERY — no shipping and handling charges ever!

WINNERS CLASSIC SWEEPSTAKES
Entry Form

YES! I want to see where passion will lead me!

Place FREE ENTRY Sticker Here

Place FREE BOOKS Sticker Here

Enter me in the sweepstakes! I have placed my FREE ENTRY sticker on the heart.

Send me six *free* Loveswept novels *and* my *free* lighted makeup case! I have placed my FREE BOOKS sticker on the heart.

Mend a broken heart. Use both stickers to get the most from this special offer!

12104

NAME_____

ADDRESS_____ APT._____

CITY_____

STATE_____ ZIP_____

Loveswept's Heartfelt Promise to You!

There's no purchase necessary to enter the sweepstakes. There is no obligation to buy when you send for your free books and lighted makeup case. You may preview each new shipment for 15 days free. If you decide against it, simply return the shipment within 15 days and owe nothing. If you keep the books, pay only $2.66 per book — a savings of over $5.00 off each shipment (plus sales tax in NY and Canada).

Prices subject to change. Orders subject to approval.
See complete sweepstakes rules at the back of this book.

CC1

ENJOY FREE HOME DELIVERY!
No shipping and no handling charges — ever!

Give in to love and see where passion leads you!
Enter the Winners Classic Sweepstakes and
send for your FREE lighted makeup case and
6 FREE Loveswept books today!

(See details inside.)

the options for a long time. Which only served to emphasize one more glaring difference between them.

Yet she couldn't deny he'd made a spectacular choice. Nor could she deny the queasy feeling that gripped her when she thought of Jack living there with someone else. Honesty compelled her to admit it wasn't the house she coveted so much as the man, a greater folly by far.

Karolyn sighed and pointed the bike toward UTMB. Her future lay in that direction, not here. No sense pining for something that was never going to happen.

By noon she'd grown thoroughly disgusted. Her hands were unsteady and she couldn't concentrate. Once, she had caught herself on the verge of botching a series of crucial measurements. The error would have corrupted the results of an important experiment. For someone who never made mistakes at work, the slipup was intolerable.

She decided to skip lunch, sit at her desk, and try to coerce her wayward brain back at least to a minimally functional level. When the phone rang, she jumped. Pepper was about the only person who ever called her here, and earlier she had begged off lunch with her friend. "Karolyn

Lucas," she said, attempting to sound efficient instead of addled.

"Did you like the gifts?"

Her mouth dropped open. Her hand flew to her throat. Seconds elapsed before she could find her voice. "Who are you?"

His short laugh sounded deep and deliciously masculine. "The man who intends to sweep you off your feet."

"Why me?"

"Because you're the woman I want."

The frank answer stole her breath, made her heart drum frantically. "How can you say that? What do you *know* about me?"

"More than you think, and less than I need to."

"Is this some kind of joke?"

"You be the judge. Do the tokens of admiration I've been sending you bear the mark of someone playing a prank?"

Lost in thought, Karolyn picked up a pencil and began doodling absently. *Exotic orchid. Box and cashews. Unusual thimble.* Expensive tokens that required thought and planning. "No," she whispered. "No, they don't."

"How would you describe them?" She detected the merest hint of a foreign accent, and though she was positive she didn't recognize his voice, there was an elusive familiarity about it.

"They were . . . very nice."

"I had hoped to impress you a little more than that."

False modesty. Everything she'd received had been tailor-made to appeal to her fantasies, as he must have known. "It's obvious you did your homework."

"Yes. I stand to gain a lot by doing this right."

"What is 'this'?" she demanded. "A game?"

"'Man is the hunter; woman is his game.'"

Her fingers tightened on the receiver. He had to be a mind reader. How else could he know she harbored a secret affinity for Tennyson? "That is a ridiculously barbaric attitude to take with a woman who has more than half a brain."

"And everyone knows Karolyn Lucas has way more than half a brain, right?" She heard him inhale, then let out a breath. "But I'm not sure all those smarts have given you any insight into the way men think."

"I'm sure no amount of smarts could do that."

The laugh again. Hearing it set off tiny ripples of excitement in her diaphragm. "Rest assured, I'm going to make sure you know exactly what I think . . . and everything I want."

She should hang up, put an end to this nonsense. Instead she heard herself ask, "How? When?"

"All in good time. I'm learning that anticipation can be a very potent aphrodisiac. Until then . . ."

"Wait! Will I—" She moistened her lips and crossed her fingers. "Will I ever find out who you are? See you?"

"Start counting the days, sweetheart."

"Gee whiz, Karo, you're a lucky duck," Pepper exclaimed as she tied a scarlet sash around the waist of her purple-and-yellow-striped workout leotard. "This secret-admirer stuff is so exciting and so-o-o romantic. Aren't you just thrilled to pieces?"

Karolyn laced up her aerobic shoes, smiling leniently at her friend's dramatic swooning. Pepper was the only person she knew who could say gee whiz and lucky duck without sounding silly. Like her nickname, the expressions reflected her personality. "I might be more thrilled if I could find out who's behind it." She had, in fact, taken Jack's suggestion and compiled a list. Not one name leaped off the page. The suspense was getting to her.

"Oh, pooh. Why not relax and enjoy the chase? Where's your spirit of adventure?"

"You're better suited to this sort of adventure than I am. I'd much rather deal with tangible evidence."

"Karolyn Lucas, I swear you're the biggest paradox. For the better part of a year you've been craving a new dimension to your life. Now that wish has come true and instead of wallowing in your good fortune, you want to dissect it like some poor pickled specimen in a biology lab." She wrinkled her nose.

"Occupational hazard, I suppose."

"I know. Both nature and training have made you analytical to a fault. I'm sure you can't help yourself."

"Thanks for being so tolerant," Karolyn said wryly.

"Hey, what are friends for?" Pepper arranged her scarlet terry sweatband and pulled on a pair of matching wrist bands. "Come on. It's time to burn, baby, burn!"

Six months before, Pepper had stepped on the scales and discovered she'd gone a few ounces over her one-hundred-pound limit. This was all the incentive she needed to enroll in an aerobics class. She had dragged Karolyn along for moral support and they'd been coming to the recreation center in Menard Park three times a week ever since.

This evening Karolyn welcomed any excuse to keep from going home, even the torture of an hour long workout led by two fitness gurus from hell. Besides, physical exertion was great for relieving stress and she had never been in better shape. Feet apart, she bent forward and stretched her arms backward between her legs.

"Don't you wonder what he looks like?" Pepper asked as she began to warm up with a series of ballet exercises.

"Mmm. I've thought about it quite a bit. Came to the conclusion he's probably your classic 'Beast' type. Either that or a little gnome of a guy who's terrified of meeting a woman in person. Why else would he carry the secrecy bit to such extremes?"

Pepper made a face while executing a graceful plié. "*I* think it's because he's one of the last true romantics, out to win the heart of his lady fair. And you know what else?" She straightened and wagged her finger accusingly. "I think deep down you're captivated, no matter how hard the cynic in you tries to disparage it."

Karolyn didn't launch into a denial because there was more than a grain of truth in Pepper's words. A small, hidden part of her did aspire to be the kind of woman who was capable of bewitching a man. So why not heed the advice and savor the exhilaration for as long as it lasted?

There was no risk of being hurt or disappointed because she knew in advance this would never progress beyond a harmless flirtation from a distance. Best of all, it had the added advantage of diverting her attention from Jack.

Starting right now, her secret admirer took top priority. *And I bet if I put my mind to it, I can beat this mystery man at his own game and figure out who he is.*

After class they showered, stopped for takeout boiled shrimp and gumbo, then went back to Pepper's apartment to watch a favorite movie on TV. The house was dark when she got home at eleven and there was no sign of Jack. Maybe he'd decided to move to his own place. That possibility plus the direct contact with her secret admirer added up to a pretty good day.

The following one didn't start out half so promising. Before her alarm went off, Karolyn was awakened by sounds coming from the adjoining bedroom. They were barely audible rustlings and she was a heavy sleeper, so she couldn't imagine why the noise had disturbed her.

She lay quietly for a few seconds, straining to

listen. Whispers? Yes . . . and a low, rumbling chuckle that sounded very suspicious. She vaulted from the bed and put her ear against the burled-walnut pocket doors that separated the bed-rooms.

Another chuckle, this one huskier and more prolonged. "Stop licking me."

"You ornery rat," she seethed. "This really tears it!" All that poppycock about gold and dross and wanting to make love with *her*. Then scant days later he'd sneaked a woman into his room. *Right under her nose!* Well, he wasn't going to get by with it. If she discovered that wanton hussy Tammy in her brother's bed, she'd boot their butts all the way to Snake Island.

Karolyn rolled the doors open with a crash, spoiling for a confrontation. "You have a lot of ner—"

"Oof, oof," a furry puppy barked at her from its perch on Jack's chest. She latched onto the edge of the door because her legs were none too steady.

"Hey, Kary. Come say hello to Sunblest Wild Weekend. I've decided to call him Rogue for short."

"How fitting." A perfect name for dog and master. "Rogue."

Hearing his name, the puppy bounded off the

bed, took an end-over-end tumble, picked himself up, and trotted toward her. She could swear he was grinning.

"He'll shake hands if you like. It's the only trick he can do right now, but the breeders promised he'll be able to learn all sorts of clever things."

"No doubt." Karolyn wasn't a dog person. To her, they were big, aggressive critters with bad breath and slobbery mouths. But this one was different. Sort of cute, cuddly, and nonthreatening. "Hi, Rogue," she said, stooping to extend her palm. He sat on his haunches, tilted his head to the side, and patted her hand with one paw.

She was a goner, and both males in the room must have recognized it. Rogue began licking her fingers and Jack laughed. "He got to me the same way. Ran straight to me, like he'd just been waiting till I showed up. At that point there was no way I could even think about choosing one of the others."

He sounded so pleased with himself, she had to smile. But when she considered how her mother would react to this little scene, the goodwill faded. "What on earth do you want with a dog in the first place?"

"For the kids. All the experts agree that pets

provide children with valuable learning experiences."

"Aren't you being a trifle premature?"

"Not really. By getting Rogue now, I'll have him all trained and adjusted before the family comes along."

"I see." She admonished herself not to let that particular subject depress her. She silently repeated the phrase "secret admirer" several times.

"Don't worry. You're gonna love having a puppy in the house."

"I can't wait for the fun to begin."

Jack sat up and rearranged the pillows so he could lean back against them. Then he meshed his fingers together behind his head. Karolyn grasped the door again and tried to regulate her breathing. His tendency to wear a minimum of clothes always left her disturbingly aware of his near nudity. Seeing him in bed, bare and sleepy-eyed, rekindled the flame of desire she had vowed to extinguish.

The pattern of hair that swept over his muscular chest held her rapt. Her fingers twitched with the need to touch the tufts under his arms, to find out if they were as silky as they looked. And her mouth went dry when she followed the tawny path that led down to where the white cotton draped low on his stomach. She licked her lips. Beneath the sheet . . .

He groaned and raised one leg. "Kary, please don't look at me that way if you're not going to do something to relieve my misery."

"I'm sorry," she blurted out, nonplussed that he'd caught her and furious that she couldn't seem to resist the inexplicable pull he exerted.

"Don't apologize. I like knowing that you're attracted to me. But you also have to understand I've been waiting for a long time and it's made me, uh . . . Well, hell, I'm hornier than I can ever remember being."

An explosion of heat bathed her, made her quiver all over. Jack waiting a long time for *her*? Hornier than he'd ever been? Right. Because the need to believe him loomed so vast and so urgent, she couldn't possibly allow herself to trust his words. "Does that line get results with most women?"

She expected him to take offense. Instead he grinned. "Don't know. You're the first one I've tried it on. Offhand, I'd say it needs a little polishing." When she crossed her arms under her breasts and glared at him, he made a futile stab at looking contrite. "Damn, Kary. All this rejection is demolishing my self-confidence."

Laughter bubbled up against her will. She

welcomed anything that broke the web of sensuality ensnaring them. "It would take a tribe of Amazons to put a dent in your ego. Even then, I wouldn't place any bets on the outcome."

Karolyn heard a whimper and traced the sound to the foot of the bed, where Rogue crouched on Jack's brand-new yellow Nikes. "Speaking of which, I hope this dog of yours came with a manual or troubleshooting instructions."

"Why?"

"'Cause he's already sprung a leak."

Jack was waiting in front of the Thompson Building when Karolyn left work that afternoon. She was surprised to see him because she'd never told him specifically where she did her research. "How did you find me?"

"Just kept opening doors and asking questions. This medical center has really expanded beyond what I remember, but it didn't take all that long to catch somebody who knew where the DNA and wound-healing study was going on."

Karolyn almost tripped stepping off the curb. She was astonished that he'd actually paid attention and remembered what she'd told him about her job. "More to the point, why did you want to find me?"

He stopped beside a shiny new moss-green Jeep illegally parked in a doctor's space. "After I got back from picking up the wagon, I went antique shopping. Found a piece that's exactly what I had in mind and left a deposit on it. But I want you to take a look, see if it's the genuine article and in good shape before I pay the rest."

She climbed up in the passenger seat, idly stroking the tan leather seat and inhaling the new-car scent while she watched him walk around to his side. He was playing havoc with yesterday's resolution to ignore him in favor of the secret admirer. True, the unknown man and his lavish gifts appealed to her tender, romantic sensibilities, but Jack stirred her emotions on a deeper, darker, more rudimentary level, a side she'd hadn't known existed.

A few presents—no matter how grand they might be—and a spectral voice paled by comparison to an in-the-flesh male, especially one as electrifying as Jack. All day long recurring images of him amid the sheets had haunted her. She just knew he'd been naked. And for a few heart-stopping seconds she had contemplated joining him there.

"Where is it?" she asked, heartened that her voice sounded normal even though her stomach was churning.

He named a dealer and headed toward the shop on Broadway. "She told me she's done business with your mother for a long time."

"Yes. Mom's bought quite a few nice pieces from her over the years. She doesn't handle anything cheap, though."

"You're telling me, but what am I gonna do? My heart's set on a certain thing and in this case I'm willing to pay for my pleasures."

Her breasts tingled and the warm feeling spiraled downward until she had to cross her legs to combat the throbbing. What was the matter with her? Almost everything he said touched off a sexual reaction. "As long as you can afford them."

He glanced at her with a bone-dissolving smile. "Don't worry. This is one pleasure that's going to be well worth the price."

A few minutes later her spirits plummeted. *Damn you, Jack.* Only a rake would have the gall to drag her here to help purchase a bed he meant to share with another woman.

But, oh, what an exquisitely fanciful bed it was, she thought with a surge of resentment. At least eight and a half feet tall, the headboard was solid all the way to the enclosed top. Both had three rows of carved panels, as did the waist-high footboard. Were it hers, she would pile it with puffy pillows and a plump comforter, perhaps even a feather bed and lushly draped hangings.

"The owner says it's right at a hundred years old," Jack murmured, seemingly as smitten by the four-poster as she was.

Karolyn bent to carefully examine the craftsmanship, calling on all the knowledge she'd absorbed from countless shopping forays and antique shows with her mother. "That's probably about right. These Elizabethan styles were fairly popular around the turn of the century." Her fingers traced the detailed carving on one of the footposts. "I'd also guess it was custom-made for a big person."

"What makes you think that?" Jack stood so close behind her, she felt the warmth of his breath on her neck. Incongrously the heat spawned a shiver.

"See how wide it is? In those days what we now call double was standard. This one looks as if it might take a king-size mattress."

"Hmm. I never thought of that, but you're right. Well, that's great. I like plenty of room to play around in, don't you?"

She heard the amusement in his taunt, knew he was baiting her, knew *he* knew her bed was the same maidenly single she'd used as a girl. "I prefer to sleep in my bed and save playing for the park."

His laugh was as naughty as her retort was prissy. "I'll bear that in mind."

"If you're intent on buying this, can we cut to the chase? I've better ways to spend my time than furnishing your love nest." Pettish on top of prissy was almost more than she could stand. Why did she keep letting him talk her into these compromising situations when she'd pledged to stay far away from him?

"By all means." He pulled a checkbook from the rear pocket of his faded jeans, removed the pen that was clipped to its cover, and studied the small tag for a few seconds. "I gave her only a hundred cash to hold it for a couple hours. So I owe the remainder of this, plus tax."

She gaped at the grossly inflated figure. "Surely you don't mean to pay full price."

"Unless you have another suggestion. I'm not in the habit of haggling over the cost when I go into a store to buy something."

Karolyn spared him a pitying glance. "Jack, if you plan on making many purchases like this, you'd better wise up. Otherwise you'll end up spending a lot more than you need to."

"Is that a fact? Like how much should I pay for this bed?"

She did a quick calculation and named an amount. He whistled through his teeth. "I knew there was more than one reason for bringing you along. So, should I just march up and tell her that's all I'll pay?"

"Would you like me to handle this end of the negotiations? You can observe and that way you'll learn how to proceed on your own next time."

He yielded to her gracefully, keeping his mouth shut while she and the shop owner went back and forth with several offers and counters until they reached a price Karolyn deemed fair. Then he dutifully wrote out the check and arranged for delivery.

Once they were outside, he put one arm around her shoulders and gave her a quick squeeze. "Thanks, Kary. You just saved me nine hundred bucks."

"I could hardly stand by and let you waste that much money."

"I appreciate your help with the bed. And to show my gratitude, you have a standing invitation to help me christen it."

SEVEN

Karolyn stopped short. Determined to rein in her temper, she said, "I beg your pardon. I must not have heard you correctly."

"Which part did you miss? The thank-you or the invitation?"

The unrepentant scoundrel! Okay, wise guy, gloves off. "Look, I've tolerated the sexual allusions and your seductive way with words, but no more. If you don't want me to boot your precious little buns out the door, you had better quit treating me this way."

"What way?"

"Like a . . . a potential conquest, one more woman in a progression of many." Another notch on his bedpost would have been literally the most appropriate accusation, but she couldn't bring herself to utter such a cliché.

He scrubbed a palm over his clean-shaven jaw. "Is that what you think I have in mind? To seduce you, then just walk away?"

"Must I spell it out in blunter terms? You've bought a house and made it clear you plan to get married soon and start a family. At first I had a hard time accepting that, but I'm beginning to believe you're serious."

"I am serious about settling down. It's the reason I came back to Galveston."

She closed her eyes for a second and took a deep breath against the rising tide of indignation. "I realize I've no right to lecture you on morals, but, Jack, shouldn't you at least *begin* your marriage with the intention of being a faithful husband?"

His head jerked up as if she'd slapped him. "What a damn fool question! Of course I intend to be a faithful husband. And not just at the beginning. Always. That's part of marriage."

He looked so ferocious and sounded so adamant, she could swear he meant what he'd said. How heavenly to have a man like Jack care so much about you and his vows that he'd willingly give up his philandering ways. Envy for that unknown woman flooded her, which in turn fueled her fury.

Hands planted on her hips, eyes narrowed,

she confronted him like an avenging angel. "Then keep your pants zipped and start acting like a man capable of fidelity. Stop propositioning me at every turn. You may have no respect for me, but damn your soul, try to show a little for your future wife."

By the time she finished the outburst, her cheeks were scorching hot and her finger jabbed him in the chest.

He caught her hand, brought it to his mouth, dropped a soft kiss on her palm. "Kary, I've said this before. I have nothing but respect for everything about you. I would never insult you with anything so crude as a proposition."

Unbidden moisture prickled in her eyes. She blinked it away. How dare he say something so sweet, kiss her so tenderly when she needed to sustain the anger as a shield. And how moronic of her to still crave the solace of his embrace.

She drew herself up ramrod straight. "Then we're in agreement? About everything?"

"I think it's safe to say we're in perfect agreement," he answered, his eyes looking dark and inscrutable. She nodded once and started to stalk away. He halted her with another admonition. "There's one thing more you should keep in mind, Kary."

He was forever telling her to "keep this in

mind" or to "remember that." "What is it this time?"

"The invitation still stands."

"There you are, dear," Mrs. Potter said from the other side of the back fence.

Preoccupied with glaring at Jack's new Jeep blocking the garage entrance, Karolyn started. "Oh, I didn't see you there. Sorry."

"Think nothing of it. You had such a faraway look, I assumed you were mentally engaged with a problem from work."

In ninety-nine cases out of a hundred, her neighbor's guess would have been accurate. This time she was busy fuming over her skirmish with Jack. *The invitation still stood to help christen his magnificent new bed.*

She'd been so enraged she had struck out to walk all the way back to UTMB for her bike. Not until he'd threatened to pick her up and stuff her in the wagon did she relent. But, as a point of honor, she had refused to talk. Nor would she speak to him when she went inside. In fact, she might never say another word to him.

"I have something for you," the tall, dignified widow said, holding up a brown paper-wrapped package. "This morning I was out front cutting roses for a bouquet when it was delivered and nobody was here. Naturally I said I'd see that you got it."

In a flash, her anger diminished, replaced by a now-familiar flutter of expectancy. Karolyn toed down her kickstand and hastened across the yard. Another enchanting treat from her secret admirer was just the diversion she needed. A touch of sweetness would go a long way toward alleviating the stress of dealing with a philistine like Jack Rowland. "Thanks for taking care of it for me."

"My pleasure, dear." Mrs. Potter passed the package over the low white pickets. "I couldn't help noticing that Jack has acquired a new vehicle and a new puppy."

"Yes," Karolyn said churlishly. "He's just one surprise after another."

Mrs. Potter beamed as a ladybug alit on one of her camellia bushes. "He confided to me last week that he plans to buy a house here in Galveston. Imagine that rapscallion settling down to a life of domesticity."

"Staggers the mind, doesn't it?"

"You shouldn't be so cynical. As a boy he was most determined to create mischief. Thirty years in the classroom taught me that determination is a trait that carries over into all endeavors. If he's made up his mind to transform into a good family man, I've no doubt he'll be an unqualified success at it."

Karolyn would rather remain a cynic. Because no matter how incensed she was with Jack, a vicious, unruly part of her hated the notion of his finding marital bliss with someone else. It was not a commendable attitude, but it existed, a painful and constant reminder that she was not the kind of woman men sought out when they were in the market for wives and children.

She sandwiched the package between her hands, clinging to it as a symbol of hope that her admirer truly would materialize soon and sweep her off her feet. Jack's eagerness to establish a home and start a family had rubbed off on her. She was driven by the need to do the same. She'd read articles about such yens. It was called the nesting instinct.

After maneuvering her bike into the garage, Karolyn trudged to the house on leaden feet. In the kitchen, she found Rogue gnawing on the mesh side of a playpen where he was confined. He yipped at the sight of her and wagged his three-inch tail in a sprightly greeting. She smiled in spite of her gloomy mood.

Ignoring Jack, who stood at the sink scrubbing russet potatoes, she lifted the adorable little bundle of fluff from his nest of shredded newspapers. "Is this what happens when you're a bad boy? You get thrown in solitary confinement?"

"I called the breeder today and she suggested the playpen for times when I don't want to take any chances. He's just ten weeks and that's a little young to be completely housebroken."

"So, my furry friend, you'd better learn to mind your manners." She transferred the puppy back to his temporary home. He was getting more excited by the minute and she didn't care to be the victim of another accident.

"I'm grilling chicken tonight. Should be ready in about thirty minutes."

"Rogue, tell your master I said you can have my portion."

Jack whipped around. "Kary, please, give me a—"

She hustled through the swinging door lest she be tempted to break her vow of silence. Jack was appallingly adept at making her forget even her best intentions.

Locked inside her room, Karolyn tore at the wrappings of her latest gift like a starving dog given a meaty bone. Come to think of it, she was almost that desperate. She uncovered a plain white box, and lifting the lid revealed a peony-pink embossed-silk drawstring bag. When she loosened the strings, a matching pink paperback book with peonies on the cover slipped out.

Her legs felt so watery, she sank into a nearby slipper chair. The romance novel was the latest by her favorite author, the one she'd meant to pick up several weeks ago. How could any stranger be so eerily in sync with her most private compulsions?

She could rationalize it away as an educated guess on his part. A large percentage of women read romances. And this writer consistently hit the best-seller lists, so anything by her was a reasonably safe choice.

Karolyn preferred to visualize her admirer as a soul mate, a man able to divine and respond to her innermost needs.

She ran her thumb over the book pages, and they separated to expose a heavy ivory card. In neat block printing the message read: *When you get to the scene on page 235, think of me making love to you that way. I want to do all those things, and more. And I want to do them soon. I can't wait much longer.*

Her fingers went numb. The note drifted to the floor. Heaven help her. She needn't turn to that page for details. She'd read enough of this author's work to know that her heroes seduced their women with masterful skill and prodigious sensuality. The illusory prince of her chaste daydreams, her fairy-tale knight, suddenly seemed every bit as threatening as Jack Rowland.

Wherever she turned, her safety was at risk, to say nothing of her sanity.

Karolyn spent the rest of the week hiding out like one of the FBI's ten most wanted. She wouldn't answer the phone, slept over on Pepper's sofa, and in general acted like the quintessential shrinking violet.

Early Saturday morning she woke up feeling miserable and displaced. "I've had it!" she announced to Pepper's kissing gourami, Mortimer Snerd. "Who's in charge of my life, anyway?"

Mort darted back and forth before pressing his mouth against the side of his bubbling aquarium. His fishy eyes stared at her, unflinching and accusatory.

"Right. Yours truly, and it's time I started acting like a woman in control."

After tidying up Pepper's living room, she biked over to the house she'd abandoned, showered in her parents' bathroom, then stole up the stairs for some clean clothes. It was barely past six and the house was quiet and dim. She breathed a little easier seeing that Jack's door was shut, but the tangibility of his presence was never far from her perception.

She pawed through her underwear drawer, bypassing those that Jack had dyed pale lavender in favor of a new pair of ivory French-cut briefs. From the satinwood clothespress she selected a daffodil-yellow short, full skirt that felt free and bouncy, a foil to the trapped sensation dogging her. A coordinating oversize yellow-and-teal top added to the illusion of freedom, as did the absence of a bra.

As a precaution, she carried her sandals, not wanting to run the risk of making any sound that would awaken Jack. Granted, she was going to have to face him sooner or later, but she needed more time to arm herself. While she crept back down the steps Karolyn debated how and where she might spend the day. But before going any-place, she wanted to read the morning *News*. They were running an article describing some of the research being done at UTMB, and she had been interviewed.

Furtively she unlocked and opened the front door, slipped on her sandals, and walked toward the curb to retrieve the paper. The sky was dark with roiling clouds and the air hung still and heavy with the portent of rain. The delivery person had wrapped the paper in clear plastic. When she picked it up, a snake uncoiled and slithered over her bare toes.

Karolyn screamed. The paper flew one way and she took off the other. In her headlong flight, she stumbled on the bottom step, clawed her way up the rest, slammed and bolted the front door, then tried to stuff her mother's valuable rug under it. It was too thick, so she spun around and clambered up the stairs, losing her footing twice.

Just as she reached the top Jack bolted out of his room, zipping his jeans on the run. He caught up with her when she dashed into her bedroom. His arms wrapped around her securely. "Kary, for Christ's sake, what's the matter? I heard you scream."

"S-sn-snake," she managed to get out between whimpers. Blanketed by chills, her whole body quaked. Drawing a breath was torture. Jack held her tighter, so close she could hear his heartbeat, feel it. She snagged his belt loops and hung on for dear life.

"A snake bit you? Show me where. No, let's get you to the hospital."

Karolyn shook her head. "Didn't . . . bite." Gulping air, she tried to speak sensibly. "It touched my toes." She shuddered again and burrowed her face into his bare chest. "Oh, Jack, I can't stand snakes."

"Shh, take it easy. You're okay now. It can't get up here." He eased her over to the bed and gently urged her to sit on it. Kneeling in front of her, he massaged her icy hands with his warm ones. "I don't know of any local snake that can climb stairs."

"I know," she said plaintively. Reality started seeping back into her consciousness, bringing with it the comprehension of how inane her fear must seem to him. If he made fun of her now, she would burst into tears for sure. She tried to withdraw her hands, but he wouldn't let them go. "I know it's completely irrational to be afraid of what was probably a little garden snake."

"To tell you the truth, I'm glad to know there's something in this world you can't master. It's downright intimidating being around such a competent woman. Makes a man feel useless."

Did he really see her as superwoman? She could have named him a hundred, a thousand things that baffled her. "But I'm a scientist. Bugs and spiders and rodents don't faze me. So why, when I see a snake, do I come unglued?"

"Hey, we all have an irrational fear or two."

"I bet you don't," she said, spoiling her stab at pluckiness with a sniffle.

"Sure I do." Seeing her question forming, he added, "No, I'm not going to tell you it yet. Can't take the chance of wrecking my manly image."

"I can't imagine anything destroying that."

"Kary," he said hoarsely, "do you want me to go see if I can find the snake? Get rid of it?"

"No."

He must have sensed something in her voice, some hint that along with the fear, her doubts about him were receding. His hands stopped their kneading. He gazed into her eyes, a penetrating, soul-searching look that chased away every rational thought. Left behind was a truth so shattering, she swayed from the impact.

She had always, always craved Jack Rowland's attention.

Even as a child she'd hung around and trailed along, enduring his teasing as the price of being close to him. Now that he was within her reach, eager and willing, she'd turned cowardly. She had done everything to discourage him, yet he remained undaunted. His famous determination.

He wanted her. And she wanted him. At this moment nothing else mattered. She hesitated, uncertain as to how she should let him know. Her concern was unfounded.

His fingers flexed, tightening around hers. "Are you sure, Kary?"

"Oh, yes."

He gave his head a little shake, as if he couldn't believe what he'd heard. "God, all of a sudden I don't know where to begin."

Suddenly she felt wise beyond her experience, and bold. "It'll probably be easier if you get a little closer."

He scrambled up to sit beside her on the bed, reaching out to brush her cheek lightly with the pads of his fingers. The gentle touch was incredibly arousing. "I've been waiting so long for this."

"How long?"

"I think all my life, really. But I got serious about it almost a year ago."

His other hand began working concurrent magic on her nape, which sent tingles racing upward to her scalp. "You mean you've been thinking about me, and our doing this for that long?"

"Longest year of my life. I don't think I could have held on many more days without going up in smoke."

She'd have expected a man so frustrated to be in a bit more of a hurry to get started. But she wasn't about to complain. His slow buildup felt wonderful. Perfect.

He blew on the vulnerable spot behind her earlobe, then gave it a leisurely bath with his tongue. The moist stroking and the warmth of his breath sent ribbons of heat streaming to every part of her body. And when his mouth finally lay claim to the sensitive skin there, her head tipped to the side, allowing him greater access.

"You taste good to me."

It was a simple declaration, but one that elated her. She meant to reply, opened her mouth, but all she could do was gasp. The sweet suction of his lips and tongue suffused her with the most extraordinary sensations. Her nipples tautened, as if his mouth were drawing on them instead of that small bit of flesh on her neck.

He had touched only there and her face, and already she was in danger of being swept away. Needing an anchor, she flexed her fingers on the denim covering his thigh. The hard muscles constricted then relaxed, an overt reminder that he'd been an athlete and had lost none of his fitness. She wanted to feel more of it, to see it. She also wanted . . .

"Jack, please kiss me. Really kiss me."

Instantly he angled her toward him, lifted her legs to drape them across his. Then his mouth was on hers, hot, open, wet—a slow and thorough exploration of every secret hidden there.

The glide of his tongue tickled the roof of her mouth, skimmed along her teeth, sought the moisture behind them. It plunged deep before withdrawing to flirt with the sensitive area just inside her lips, an eternal, alternating pattern that made her body undulate to the same rhythm.

When she had daringly asked for the kiss,

she'd had no concept of how deep and tempestuous Jack could make an act that she had always found overrated. Now she knew, and if the pulsing changes in her femininity were any clue, he was about to introduce her to even more delectable surprises. Especially since he'd shifted her fully onto his lap and positioned her to face him with her legs cradling the outside of his.

The dressing-table mirror reflected a scandalously posed woman with swollen lips and slumberous eyes, sinking her nails into broad, masculine shoulders. The sight of them so provocatively entwined heated her blood, sent it coursing through her veins like volcanic overflow.

Fingers spread, his hands slipped beneath her loose-fitting top and began a slow climb from her waist, skipping lightly over each rib and coming to rest before reaching her breasts. Karolyn arched, silently imploring him to ease the heaviness he'd created there. Like a fantasy lover, Jack understood her slightest demand and hastened to fulfill it.

He thumbed the hem of her top upward, and unable to wait for him to free her of it completely, she leaned into him, rubbing her breasts against the soft, stimulating hair on his chest. The bonding was so pleasing, yet so piercing, a wanton cry escaped before she could swallow it. He took care of that, matching the sound with a hungry groan and muttered words of approval.

While his palms smoothed up and down her thighs they moved against each other in graceful, erotic counterpoint. She loved their contrasting shapes and textures, loved the billowy feeling of floating above herself. Most of all she loved fitting the very center of her to the hard, thrusting pressure of his arousal, hearing his raspy struggle for breath, and abandoning herself to her own heightened sensuality.

Karolyn had never reached this plateau of sexual excitation, never been so close to . . . She moved faster.

"Kary, sweetheart, here." He stood, swiveled, and bent to place her on the bed.

When he straightened, her arms fell away from him, leaving her disappointed and bereft. She needed reassurance. Suddenly self-conscious about her near nudity, she grabbed a pillow and held it against her chest. "Didn't you like what we were doing?"

"I think you know I did." He glanced down at the front of his jeans. "Do."

She glanced down for confirmation. "Then why—"

"Another hazard of waiting so long, I'm afraid. Everything was about to come to a crash-

ing conclusion, and me still with my pants on."
He gave her a rueful smile. "I had sort of visualized a different ending."

"Oh," she whispered, relieved that she hadn't committed some unpardonable blunder. He'd led her into alien territory and she was literally feeling her way. But she had liked the feel of it. "In that case, what's next?"

Jack chuckled and put one knee on the bed. "This." He swept aside her protective pillow and, along with several others, tucked it behind her so that she was half reclining. "This." He snagged the elastic waistband of her skirt and worked it slowly over her hips and down her legs, then tossed it to the floor. "And this." His thumbs and middle fingers encircled her ankles, then separated to chart a sinuous ascent until her briefs met the same fate as her skirt.

"Now lie back. I want to look at you."

Totally exposed to his ardent gaze, she stirred restlessly. The briefly banked flames he'd kindled deep within her burst to life. His intensity was at once thrilling and disconcerting. "Unfair advantage." She reached for his zipper; he brushed her hand aside.

"I'll make sure you get your turn. Soon. But first . . ." He used his mouth to track the same course his hands had only moments ago. His touch on her skin drew the internal flames to the surface, and she writhed in their fiery wake.

When he knelt astride her, supporting his weight on both elbows, and sucked her nipple deep into his mouth, she moaned and bowed her back completely off the bed. His tongue flicked and circled the peak until, satisfied with the hardness and shape of it, he shifted to bestow equal attention on her other breast. All her sensory receptors merged at those twin pleasure points, luring her with a shimmering glimpse of fulfillment.

"Jack," she said breathlessly, "I'm melting."

One finger slipped between her legs then, probed delicately, and found her damp and sleek. Ready. "Yes, almost. I *want* you to melt for me. All the way."

Poised on the brink of ecstasy, she stepped back. "Only if you're with me."

"Later. I want to give you—"

"Not without you."

He swore, but his control was apparently as tenuous as hers. He wrestled himself out of his jeans, dug in a pocket, and held up a condom. "Do you want me to use this, Kary?"

She hesitated, a few seconds of madness, while she battled the need to grasp whatever reward fate would allow her from their union. In the end, sanity won out. She nodded, whispered,

"Yes," and extended both hands to cover him as he rolled on the protection.

"This time," he said softly.

She barely heard. Her hands measured the length and thickness of him, guided it to the portal of her most private place, and urged him to claim what he wanted. "Take me."

"God, Kary. God." He entered her with a long, fluid thrust that left both of them panting for breath.

Invaded. Possessed. Seconds ticked by while she adjusted to the reality of them locked together, of Jack filling her so completely. Her wildest fantasies hadn't prepared her for such bliss.

Then he said, "I love being inside you," and she was lost. "I don't want to let you go. Ever." He began to move, reaching between them to touch her, just above where they were joined.

She was soaring, wings spread, caught on an updraft that pushed her higher and higher. His breath hit her face, her neck, her ear, like a hot wind from the Gulf. "Come with me, Kary."

"Yes!"

Her body buckled, racked by one convulsive spasm after another until she was so spent all she could do was cleave mindlessly to Jack and sob his name in joy and surrender while she gloried in the explosive power of his release.

They lay facing each other on the narrow bed. "I thought you were never going to shed those jeans. Kind of peculiar after all those times you paraded around in front of me wearing a lot less."

"I knew once the pants were gone, I would be too."

Karolyn rubbed her nose against the damp muskiness of his chest, darted her tongue out to wash his nipple. It beaded so satisfactorily, she did the other.

"You're a temptress, Kary Lucas."

A temptress. No man had ever called her that. None of the academic accolades, not even the international science award, had filled her with as much pride as Jack's praise. And she had never been as unabashedly happy as she was at this moment. "Was what happened so bad?"

"Not when you consider that we have a long, lazy day ahead of us." Right on cue, rain began falling on the roof. "See?"

"I take it you have some rainy-day recreation in mind."

"Mmm. Looks to me like a day to curl up in bed with a good book." He was still inside her and vitally alive. "Or with someone who's read a good book recently."

— ❦ ————————— ❦ —

"Let's take a nap."

She poked him playfully in the ribs. "What's the matter? All the exertion wear you out?"

He imprisoned her hand. "No. I haven't slept very well the past few nights, wondering where you were. And with whom."

"Jealous?"

"Yes."

The stark confession left her speechless. She was not the sort of woman to inspire such primal reactions in a man. "Okay," she agreed at last. "I haven't slept all that well myself."

They lay in silence for a long, lazy time, listening to the rain. "Jack?"

"Mmm?"

"I can fall asleep only on my right side."

"No problem." He nestled her back against his chest, spoon fashion. "Good thing I'm left-handed, huh?"

Oh, that left hand was clever as sin. She moaned.

It was a long time before they got any sleep.

EIGHT

She had let him get her much too deeply involved . . . with both him and his house project.

"What do you think? The light one?" Paintbrush in hand, Jack stepped back from a pair of
sawhorses in the doorway of his garage. Across
them spanned a length of wood he was using to
test various stain samples.

"You might want to consider going with a
darker shade for the woodwork. It'll blend better
with your bed." Karolyn had schooled herself not
to do much reflecting on that particular piece of
furniture. Its imposing presence in his big, high-
ceilinged bedroom conjured up too many memories
of how they had spent the better part of yesterday.

She still had a hard time believing Jack's love-
making wasn't a product of her dreams.

"Why didn't it occur to me that the wood

colors should complement each other?" He shook his head. "I obviously have a lot to learn about putting a house together so it looks right. That's why I need you to advise me."

More than once she had tried to bow out of that job, but her protests fell on deaf ears. When Jack Rowland wanted something, he just assumed he was going to get it sooner or later. She sighed. So far he'd been right. "I'm sure it'll all start falling into place. You've barely begun." Significantly he had chosen to complete the master bedroom first.

"Yeah, but I'm still going to rely on your judgment about a lot of things. We'll be a team. You provide the brains and I supply the sweat equity." He swiped at the rivulets running down his chest, dried his damp hand on the front of his purple shorts.

Karolyn's throat felt as if she'd swallowed a cotton ball. She rested her hips on the edge of a large wooden packing crate and clamped her legs together. By unleashing her passion, Jack had seemingly converted her from asexual to insatiable. She focused on the backyard arbor. All that did was remind her that he had wanted to make love there, surrounded by the roses. Now she wanted to as well.

Knowing what she knew now, would she have

made a different decision early Saturday morning? She couldn't say. One thing was certain. Giving in to her fascination for Jack had changed her life immeasurably. It also left her with a truck-load of doubts.

He apparently did not share her misgivings. He'd awakened with a huge smile on his face, made very energetic love to her, and sung in the shower. Then he had insisted they go out for an enormous coffee-shop breakfast. Now he was whistling a Sousa march as he dabbled with the paintbrush.

"You act as if you haven't a care in the world beyond picking that stain."

He either didn't pick up on her surliness or chose to ignore it because he grinned. "Kary, my sweet, why shouldn't I be happy? Everything is working out just the way I want it to."

My sweet? She tried not to be flattered by the endearment, but living the fantasy won out and she made the most of it. "Working out with the house, you mean?"

He carried the piece of wood over for her final approval. "That's part of it. But mostly I'm just pleased and satisfied with my life in general. Should have come back years ago."

Had he done that, she'd have missed the chance to attract his attention, even fleetingly.

"Well, I hope you're always as happy as you are right now." Brave words.

"Don't worry. I've no doubt that for me, things are going to get a whole lot better." He planted a quick kiss on her forehead. "Very soon."

And for her, things would no doubt get infinitely worse. In the meantime she wasn't going to mope around waiting for the ax to fall. She was a mature woman who'd made the decision to buy a ticket, and she was going to ride her train to the end of the line. Karolyn cringed. Clichés were so trite. Probably the reason they sprang to mind so readily.

She tapped her finger on a medium-dark oak stain. "This is definitely the one you want. And be sure to use a matte finish to seal it. Otherwise it'll look too glossy and modern."

"Okay. I'll pick up a couple gallons of both first thing in the morning. Now let's go back upstairs. I want to see what ideas you have for the walls."

She had mixed emotions about getting any more enmeshed in his redecoration project. In some ways it would be torture. Conversely, it was such a lovely old house and she didn't want to see the job botched. Too, there was the small matter of pride. Leaving her indelible mark on Jack's home might ensure that he would never be able to forget her completely. Besides, he had insisted she do it.

Karolyn, you have to be sick to rationalize something so bizarre. Nevertheless she climbed the stairs with a renewed sense of purpose.

While she'd been avoiding him by hiding out he had been a busy little worker bee. In addition to picking up his Jeep, making several trips to the Port of Houston to collect crates he'd had shipped from various parts of the world, and antique shopping, he had refinished the bedroom floor and stripped and sanded the woodwork. "You must have put in some long hours to accomplish so much in a week."

"Yep. I'm trying to make this place livable as quickly as possible. But I also want to do as much of the work as I can myself." He ran a hand over the beaded millwork. She had to admit he was showing all the signs of pride of ownership.

"You're anxious to move in, then?"

"What's the matter? In a hurry to get rid of me?"

A week ago she would have rejoiced at the prospect. Today the likelihood left her gloomy. "I understand why you'd be eager to have a place of your own."

"You know, I really am looking forward to

being a part of this neighborhood. Every day I was here working, at least one person stopped by to chat."

"You have to remember, Galveston is basically a small town. People are friendly."

"True, but I took care of some business at the same time. A rep from the East End Historical District Association—by the way, I'm automatically a member by owning property here—told me they have block parties, May Day celebrations, Christmas caroling, and all kinds of activities for residents."

"I'm sure you'll fit right in." Drat! She had to stop sounding so petulant and feeling so excluded. If she started getting proprietary about man or house, she was headed for disaster.

"Then one of the neighbors who's lived next door since the thirties filled me in on the background of this house. Nicholas Clayton's daughter said he designed it, but no corroborating evidence has been found. So, although we can't claim it's a Clayton, I'm still pretty excited."

"I can tell."

He paced around the room checking out every minor detail, like a curious child with a new toy.

"Guess what else? The original owner was a sea captain who had a fear of storms. When the hurricane warnings went up in 1900, he took his family to a ship in the harbor and they rode out the storm safely while over six thousand people were killed on the island. The house survived intact too." He looked at her, wonder lighting those blue, blue eyes. "This sucker is built to withstand anything, and my family is going to live in it. Isn't that great to know?"

"Uh, yes, great. Very reassuring."

"I've also joined the Galveston Historical Foundation and one of the ladies asked if I'd be interested in having the house included on their homes tour in May. Do you think I ought to agree?"

"Depends on how you feel about five thousand strangers trooping through your house on two successive weekends."

Jack dropped down to sit cross-legged on the floor in front of one the tall windows. He looked good backlit by sunshine. "Hmm. Never thought about it that way. Maybe it's not such a good idea, after all. I was thinking more along the lines of showing off what we'll have done by then."

For all of two seconds Karolyn felt a matching spurt of satisfaction. Then she remembered that his "we" didn't include her. "Suit yourself," she said nonchalantly, and wedged herself in a corner.

"No, this is going to be a home by then, not a museum. Privacy is more important."

"Right." He and his bride would figuratively still be on their honeymoon next May. Again she wondered if her much-ballyhooed brains had turned to saw dust. "So what's your question about the walls?"

"Well, I bought a whole bunch of books on residential preservation and one is on the unusual color combinations they used for Victorian exteriors, which is something else we have to deal with later. I'm wondering if they painted the insides those odd colors."

"Some of them probably did. But that doesn't mean you have to. Stick to whatever you like. You also could go with wallpaper, at least in some of the rooms. It adds a lot of character without costing a fortune."

He scanned all four walls, as if trying to visualize them covered. "You think paper would look good in here?"

"Yes." She pulled in her bottom lip, chewed on it for a moment before adding, "If it were going to be my room, I'd hang a nice tailored pattern in a dark color, then choose a more detailed fabric for the bed and upholstery."

"Good enough. You name the time and we'll go pick out everything we need."

Later that evening as Karolyn formed the burgers Jack was going to cook on the grill, she reflected on the day. It had been strange in a way. He had started it off with a dazzling display of passion. She had little basis for comparison, but she didn't need the Ph.D. to figure out that he was everything a woman could hope for in a lover.

Oddly enough, for the remainder of the day, he seemed content just to be with her, to have her input on his work with the house. Gone were the see-through-you looks and the innuendos. Oh, he touched her, naturally and often, even kissed her several times, but there was no suppressed tension, no urgency. It was if a pressure valve had been released, leaving them free to be comfortable with each other and to communicate on a level beyond the sexual attraction.

That part hadn't diminished, at least not for her and she didn't think for him either, but now it was manageable. For lack of a better description, they had filled their day with togetherness, easy conversation, shared interests, and good sex. Much as she imagined happily married young couples did.

The tomato she had picked up to slice popped from her grasp and the knife wobbled dangerously. *Married?* Time for another reality check. She and Jack were engaged in a brief affair between mutually consenting adults. Mustn't give it more import than it deserved. Marriage was in his future, not hers.

She steadied herself and, with a scientist's precision, began making straight, measured cuts in the tomato her neighbor had grown.

The backdoor flew open, bringing in a gust of warm air, the aroma of charcoal smoke, and Jack. "Burgers ready for the fire?"

"Ready." She was determined to carry this off with a savoir faire befitting her intelligence. "Let's eat in the dining room for a change. We'll use the china and crystal and sterling. Light candles and borrow a bottle of Dad's Château Margaux. He saves those for the celebrations like births and promotions and—"

"Weddings?" Strong arms slipped around her waist from behind. Wrists crossed, he lifted her breasts so that his breath tickled the cleavage when he nuzzled her neck. "Sounds good." His tongue did decadent, debilitating things to her ear. "Know what I'd like better?"

She shook her head. It only increased the maddening friction.

"I'd like to wolf down the food real fast, maybe even forget about it, and take the wine to bed with us. We can do our celebrating there."

"Did you enjoy your weekend?"

That voice! Starting guiltily, Karolyn juggled the phone. How did her secret admirer know when she would be alone at lunchtime? It had been several days since she'd heard from him, and in spite of her decision to concentrate on the mystery man, Jack had dominated her thoughts. Telling herself she owed no allegiance to this disembodied stranger didn't free her from a vague feeling that she'd somehow betrayed him. "It was very nice."

That laugh! Wicked and seductive, reminding her of last night. She had spent it in Jack's bed and "naughty" was a more suitable term to describe what he had done to her, taught her to do to him. She closed her eyes and trembled at the recollection. He had wasted no time in filling the gaps in that area of her education.

"Before long, I'm going to make sure your weekends are better than nice. We'll be spending all of them together. I'm getting turned on just thinking about it."

"Please, you shouldn't say things like that to me."

"Why not? It's true. Don't you think a man and a woman should always be honest with each other, whether they are friends . . . or lovers?"

"Well, yes," she hedged. Honesty was a fine ideal. In real life there were times when it was impossible to tell the whole truth. "But we're neither friends nor lovers. I don't know you and—"

"You do. You're just not trying hard enough to figure out who I really am. My gifts have all been right on target, haven't they? Who could possibly know your tastes well enough to pick them expressly for you?"

"Don't you think I've tried to guess that?" she almost shouted. "Everybody male I work with is starting to give me peculiar looks because I've been surreptitiously eyeing them, asking quirky questions to see if somebody will trip up and reveal himself."

"Has it worked?"

"No," she said tartly. "You know it hasn't. The truth is, I don't think these men around here are imaginative enough to go to the lengths you have."

"I'll take that as a compliment to my tenacity. Have you tried looking elsewhere, beyond where you work?"

"I've done that too. My best friend's brother laughed uproariously when I confronted him point-blank. A couple of the guys in my aerobics class thought I was trying to pick them up. They're so self-absorbed, they would naturally assume that."

He chuckled, then in his barely detectable foreign accent asked, "Anyone else?"

Only every male she could think of between nine and ninety, including the most unlikely Jack Rowland. "Believe me, I've racked my brain. You're driving me crazy, you know. How much longer are you going to subject me to this torment?"

"My aim is to charm you, to intrigue and enthrall, not torment. I only want you to be as excited about our coming together as I am. It won't be much longer, I promise. I'm marking the days off on my calendar, and dreaming about you every night."

He hung up without saying good-bye. Karolyn slammed down the receiver in frustration. His cat-and-mouse game was a distraction she didn't need, especially when her emotions and priorities were in such a tangle.

She was balanced on a tightrope, desire for Jack warring with the inevitable pain losing him would bring. Now the secret admirer was promising to get into the act, a further complication. *I'm marking the days off on my calendar.*

Karolyn slid her own desktop calendar toward

her. She had another sword hanging over her head. If she was going to put her name in competition for that professorship, she had to do it before the start of Labor Day holiday next weekend. She wished she could be more decisive. Always before she'd had a clear sense of direction, about what she wanted and how to get it. In this, she could only vacillate.

Pepper was pushing her to go for it. But even Pepper didn't know about her secret fear. No one did. She couldn't bring herself to confess. It was too dumb.

Just as it was dumb to go rushing home from work at the earliest plausible moment. She didn't even waste time defending her haste. She wanted to see Jack, pure and simple.

Karolyn had expected to find him at the house on Postoffice, but there was no sign of his Jeep and all the doors were locked. She didn't know what made her use the key he had urged her to take. Masochism maybe, but something drew her inside and up the stairs.

The unmistakable smell of paint and solvents lingered, but it wasn't unpleasant. In the seventies, the house had been converted to a central-air-conditioning system and the first thing Jack did was to upgrade the wiring and install new dual-zone units. Unlike her parents' house, up-stairs here was as cool and comfortable as down.

When she reached the doorway of the master bedroom, she froze, fingers curling around the jamb. A sharp pain pierced her heart. The four-poster stood squarely in the center of the room to allow space for the finishing touches on walls and woodwork.

As if magnetized, the bed pulled at her. A mattress and springs had been delivered that day, and on them was a set of sheets, neatly tucked, folded, and turned down. Ready.

She ran a finger over the crisp cotton. Dark blue to match his eyes. Her own misted, but she refused to shed tears. Instead she dashed from the room, down the stairs, and out the backdoor to claim her bike. She absolutely would never share that bed with Jack. She had knowingly compro-mised her principles for the sake of their affair, would probably continue the lunacy for a brief time, so powerful was her need for him.

But there had to be a limit and she drew the line at sleeping in another woman's bridal bed. What an unholy mess.

By the time she pedaled to her home, Karolyn had done a fair job of brainwashing herself. She wasn't going to tell Jack about her detour. Nor would she stage a big scene if he tried to entice her into christening the bed. She would simply refuse. End of discussion.

"Hi, Kary." Jack greeted her a second before Rogue chimed in with a couple of welcoming yips. The puppy definitely had a winning personality. He was smart and fun to have around. Maybe she'd get one of her own when Jack took him and moved out. Where once she had relished her solitude, now she dreaded the thought of being left alone.

"Hello, you two," she said, struggling to sound jovial. "What mischief did you stir up today?"

"Tell her you developed a taste for wood and chewed off the spindly legs on that little gold stool in the entry hall."

"Good Lord, Jack! Mom will have all our heads. That piece is, was, over two hundred years old. They're hard to find and she sank a mint into it." Scratch the idea of a puppy, at least until she moved out of here.

"Don't go ballistic. I was kidding. I got there in time to rescue her precious stool, but it's a fact Rogue loves to gnaw on wood, kinda like babies and teething rings." He stopped to pick up what looked like a stair baluster. "So I took him to a millwork place and let him choose a toy."

"Do me a favor and joke about something

besides my mother's antiques." She was too relieved to be unduly distressed that he knew about
such things as teething rings. Had he stocked up
on baby books at the same time he bought all
those volumes on remodeling?

"That's why I thought you might be interested in going along with us tonight."

"To where?"

"I've enrolled in dog-obedience classes. The
teacher says he's really too young, but what the
heck. Anything he learns will be an improvement.
We can't have him chewing on the furniture and
piddling on the Oriental rugs, now can we?"

"Not in *this* house, we can't."

"So you'll go to the first class with us?"

She was almost as much of a sucker for the dog
as for its master. And neither would be around for
much longer. "Sure, why not?"

"Good. We need to take off right now, is that
okay? The class lasts only an hour, and we can
pick up something to eat on the way back."

With the aid of a rawhide chew they coaxed
the puppy into a sky kennel that was much too
large for him. "Is he going to grow big enough to
fill this thing?" It took up a good portion of the
Jeep's rear cargo compartment.

"No, he'll weigh less than twenty pounds full
grown. I just wanted him to have room to move

around some. I'd hate to be locked in a cage, even for a short time."

Karolyn remembered what her grandmother used to say about a crabby old man who lived in her neighborhood. All the kids thought he was an ogre. But Grandma said anybody who loved and took care of his animals like that man did had to have a kind soul. Her heart softened a little more when she realized her grandmother would say the same thing about Jack.

The woman conducting the classes lived on acreage several miles past the state park on Termini–San Luis Pass Road. Karolyn rarely ventured down to the western end of the island. This evening she was enjoying the drive, listening to Jack report at length on the progress he'd made that day, and calling out encouragement to Rogue. Though she was poised to rebuke any sly references to the bed, he didn't mention it. Perhaps, like last night, he meant to save his suggestions until he could act on them.

Karolyn, you are hopeless, shameless.

As soon as Jack had parked, he released Rogue from his carrier. The puppy woofed and ran in circles around him, nipping at his heels. "I guess he's decided not to hold a grudge against me, after all. Maybe he didn't mind being crated."

Hearing the commotion, the teacher came

around the end of an aluminum outbuilding. She hunkered down to address the puppy, who lifted his paw on cue. "My, aren't you a smart young man. And so handsome. You have champion written all over you."

Like a true showman, Rogue pranced and strutted, accepting the lavish compliments as his due. All three humans laughed, which caused him to ham it up even more outrageously.

The teacher stood and said, "You must be Jack Rowland."

"Right." He shook the offered hand.

"And this is Mrs. Rowland?"

"No, uh, no. This is my, uh, she's, um. This is Kary Lucas."

Karolyn smiled tolerantly and offered her hand to the woman. Jack's clumsy introduction puzzled her. Obstinate as he'd been as a child, his mother had somehow managed to inculcate him with proper manners. He was normally very adept in social situations, much smoother than Karolyn. Why had he stumbled over a simple introduction?

The question stayed on her mind for the duration of the lesson. Rogue, while charming, enthusiastic, and funny, was by no means a star pupil. If not for the fact that he learned to sit on command, he'd have been a washout.

"Don't worry," the teacher consoled afterward. "As I told you, he's young. But smart and eager. He'll shape up eventually."

"He did so well at first," Karolyn declared.

"They pick up the 'sits' fairly easily. The 'stays' take a bit more time. And the 'comes' are the hardest part of all."

Behind the teacher, Jack wiggled his brows at Karolyn and showed her a grin that was indisputably lascivious. Then he shook his head and mouthed, "Not for me."

She stuck her tongue out at him. Thankfully the teacher had bent to bid Rogue farewell.

They stopped at a disreputable-looking roadside joint and got takeout to eat on the beach at a nearby pocket park. The ribs were messy, but delicious. Rogue chased a tennis ball and sniffed suspiciously at the surf. But after a couple of screeching halts at the waterline, he finally relented and got his feet wet. Then he dug into the sand and raced back to them, as if expecting them to praise his bravery. And, of course, they did.

Pensive on the drive back, Karolyn wondered if Jack would take to parenting as readily as he had to raising and caring for the puppy. Some instinct told her he would.

When he'd showed up on her doorstep not so long ago, she had classified him as what her Regency novels called a rakehell. But her opinion of him had undergone a gradual shift. Something had inspired a drastic change in him. She now believed he would carry out his plan to establish a home, find a wife, and start a family. The sooner the better.

It was her misfortune that when he got serious about the latter two items on his list, he would, out of necessity, need to look elsewhere.

Her misfortune, too, that she had fallen in love with him.

NINE

Karolyn held her breath as she ascended the stairs, her senses alive with the awareness that Jack followed close behind. Like a married couple preparing to retire for the night. No! She had to stop making those inappropriate comparisons. To use Jack's word, they were cohabiting. She reeled, grabbed for the railing to brace herself. At first cohabiting sounded merely risqué, forbidden. Now it sounded sordid.

His hand fastened on her waist. "Is something wrong, Kary?"

Nothing, apart from a case of unrequited love. "I'm fine. Just a little tired." And on edge about spending another night in his arms. Did he expect it? Did she want it? How much longer could she keep up this charade?

"I haven't been letting you get enough sleep. I'm sorry. I'll do better tonight."

She wanted to scream and didn't quite know why. Instead she repeated firmly, "I'm fine. Don't worry about me."

"It isn't worry exactly. More like concern. I just want to take good care of you."

That made her sad and angry at the same time, and more determined than ever not to depend on him for anything. "I've been taking care of myself for a long time. There's no reason I can't continue to do so."

Her let her flash of assertiveness pass. "By the way, a package came for you right before you got home. In the confusion of getting away for Rogue's lesson, I forgot to tell you. I left it on your bed."

She stepped up the pace to her room, anxious for a diversion. Lying on her pillow was a large envelope; inside it a portfolio in the most delectable shade of yellow. She trailed her fingers over the leather, found it fantastically soft. She adored the heady scent and sensual texture of soft leather.

"Well, I have to hand it to the guy. He's persistent."

Karolyn shook herself back to reality. "Yes, and he has fabulous taste." She clicked open the gold snap and in the center compartment, wrapped in gold foil, was a calendar for the coming year. The cover featured gorgeous artwork with a Victorian theme.

Jack leaned against the door frame, arms crossed. "The leather thing looks okay, but why a calendar?"

Perplexed, she flipped to January. In small, neat letters on the first was the message: *I want to dance with you until we drink a champagne toast at midnight. After that, we'll make love to welcome in the first of many New Years we will spend together.*

She touched her lips, her heart. Her chest constricted with wrenching emotion. When Jack had predicted the secret admirer might heat things up, she had dismissed it as farfetched. But for the first time gut instinct told her this enigmatic stranger might be serious after all.

She continued to turn the pages. Every month had notations about Galveston special events they would share—Mardi Gras in February, the blessing of the Mosquito Fleet after Easter, beach cleanup in September, the November Jazz Fest, and Dickens on the Strand in December.

Karolyn tucked the calendar out of sight in the folio, cradled it closely, and closed her eyes. Like a precious promise of hope, she wanted to protect and nurture it. Jack offered no such promise of hope for the future, but this man, with his insightful gifts and his sentimental nature, called to her as a kindred spirit. Surely they shared a mystical link.

He spoke of making love. With him, it would be sweet and ethereally romantic. Not at all like the dark, all-consuming passion she'd discovered with Jack. Yes, she thought, clinging more tightly to the leather. This was the sort of man on whom she should pin her future.

"Kary?"

She opened her eyes, shocked to find Jack looming over her. "Yes?" she asked dreamily.

"What did that calendar have in it that sent you off to another planet?"

"Nothing that would interest you." She rose and pulled back the covers on her bed. "I think you were right. I do need to get some sleep. I hope you don't mind if I say good night now."

For long moments he looked so menacing she was afraid he wasn't going to accept her symbolic slam of the bedroom door in his face. Then the ghost of a smile flitted over his lips. "I understand, sweetheart. I'll leave you to your dreams."

She drifted off to sleep with only the germ of an idea disrupting her reverie. Why did his use of "sweetheart" seem so out of place?"

Jack parked the Jeep in a visitors' lot and checked his watch. He'd accomplished virtually nothing all morning aside from grappling with doubts over the wisdom of what he was about to do. Telling himself it was unnecessary and idiotic, that it could cost him in countless ways hadn't deterred him in the end.

He had launched a two-pronged attack and it was vital to secure both flanks. He winced at the military analogy. Kary sure wouldn't take kindly to a courtship patterned along the lines of a battle campaign. But last night one of his flanks had been outmanned and today he was going to move in reinforcements.

Now, if fate would only cooperate and deliver him Kary alone. He knew the building, but not her office number, so he had to ask directions. As he came down the hall her door opened. A stoop-shouldered man wearing a comical straw boater and a white lab coat with a name tag identifying him as Bernard hurried out, muttering something about a meeting as he passed Jack in the hall.

Jack crossed his fingers and reached for the knob, turning it slowly. She was alone, poring over a computer printout on her desk. He released the breath he'd been holding. So far so good.

Instead of the contacts that he knew sometimes bothered her, a pair of glasses perched on her tipped-up nose. "There's a knack to looking professional and cute at the same time." She did a heck of a lot more for her lab coat than Bernard had. No matter what she wore, she did a heck of a lot for him.

Her head snapped up. She shot out of the chair. "What are you doing here?"

"I want you."

He hadn't moved, but she started backing up. "W-want me? For what?"

"Don't be dense, Kary. You know for what."

With their gazes meshed, he saw the instant when what he'd said sank in. Her eyes widened above the glasses. She shook her head. "Jack, don't even think about doing that here."

"It's all I *can* think about." He began a steady advance.

She threw up a warning hand and took a backward step for each one of his. "I refuse to be party to anything so insane."

"It isn't the same without your participation. Trust me, I know what I'm talking about on that score."

"Trust you? Not likely." Her back hit the wall. "You're crazy. Wild."

He closed in, penned her by planting his

palms flat against the wall on either side of her head. "Not yet. But hold on, sweetheart, I'm fixin' to show you wild."

His lips smothered her protest, swooping down to capture hers with a devouring kiss. She defied him a little at first, but he held her fast and wooed her with every bit of the love and affection and respect that filled his heart. And he silently begged for her to return it in full measure.

He must have communicated his message clearly, because like kindling touched by a spark she caught fire, burning slowly at first, then hotter and hotter until they were both panting and climbing all over each other.

He carried her to the desk and set her on the edge, removed the glasses, then insinuated himself between her legs. "Jack, please, what if someone—"

"Comes in here? I'm counting on it." He drowned out this protest with another no-holds-barred kiss that went on and on, enveloping them in a voluptuous haze.

She wasn't wearing stockings under her skirt. That excited him unbearably. The skin of her inner thigh felt like heaven as his hand slid inexorably upward, until at last he reached the damp heat that nearly undid him. "Oh, Kary. Nothing on earth feels this good."

When she breathed a muted sound of sanction, he felt like shouting. She wanted him as much as he wanted her. That realization made the blood sizzle in his veins, drove him to dizzying heights.

"I can't wait. Sorry." His voice vibrated into her mouth as he fumbled ineptly with her underpants and the zipper of his jeans. His thumb and forefinger touched that sweet, secret place. He groaned. God, she was so hot, so wet. He was drowning in the scent and feel of her.

Knowing he was handling her too fast and too roughly didn't slow him down one iota. At that point a gun held to his head wouldn't have made any difference. Desperation made him reckless. He forged into her, as deep as he could reach, exulting in the initial resistance, then the engulfing acceptance.

She didn't seem to notice his lack of finesse. Her fingers grasped and tugged at his hair so fiercely that his eyes watered. Her legs locked around his waist. She murmured in his ear, exhorting him into a frenzied rhythm that sent his excruciating need spiraling so high all he could do was let the pounding force of his release erupt within her.

Jack heard the ragged, agonized rasp of his breathing and, mercifully, felt the pulses of her orgasm contract around him. He collapsed against her. His clothes were soaked. His heart pumped like a bellows. He was certain he would never be able to move again.

Somewhere close to his ear, his watch ticked off minutes while they recovered.

Kary was the first to speak. "I was right. So was Mrs. Potter. You are a rascal and a rogue, a rake and a rapscallion."

Jack chuckled. Damn, he felt good. Weak but good. "Why, thank you, ma'am."

"Those weren't meant as compliments."

He kissed the side of her neck, her throat, her chin. "I'm accepting only compliments today. File your complaints on Monday."

"Yesterday was Monday."

"Mmm." This time his mouth lingered on her nose, cheeks, forehead. "I have a whole week to get back in your good graces."

Kary pushed him away and struggled to her feet. "What I'm worried about right now is how I'm going to get through the rest of today."

"I don't know about you, but I am definitely going to get through it with a smile on my face." He demonstrated.

"If I had the strength, I'd smack your self-satisfied smile clear into next week." She attempted to smooth her skirt, then reached down for her panties. "For heaven's sake, Jack, zip up your jeans and do something about your hair. You look disreputable, disgraceful."

"And you look . . ." He whispered the rest in her ear.

"Get out of here!"

"All right, all right. I'm going."

He was almost to the door when she halted him. "There was more to that than just wanting me, Jack."

She hadn't asked it as question, but he was happy to oblige her with an answer. "I think of it as reaffirming a prior claim. You're starting to get real enamored of this phantom and his sappy gifts. All I wanted was to remind you what it's like to make love with a real man, face-to-face."

"That is disgusting! You used me to satisfy an imbecilic macho urge, to prove you hold some power over me."

"No more than you used me. If you really wanted to stop me, you could have, and I think you know it. So what were *you* out to prove, Kary?"

Imperiously she aimed a finger at him. "This time I mean it. Go."

He went.

By the time he reached the Jeep, his smile had vanished and the euphoria was evaporating almost as fast. He'd been so sure that taking Kary by storm would strengthen his claim on her. Jack had devised the strategy to guarantee that *he*, not the secret admirer, ranked foremost in her thoughts.

Both hands gripping the wheel, he replayed her accusations while he drove slowly toward downtown. Had he, in fact, been motivated by an imbecilic macho urge to prove he held power over her? No, not exactly, and not consciously. But he found the real reason for his actions even less palatable.

Only an idiot would fabricate a fantasy man, then get rabidly jealous of his own creation. So jealous that he had come on like a Neanderthal . . . like a macho imbecile. Kary had called him crazy, wild. She'd been right. At the time he had convinced himself that her passion equaled his own. What if she remembered it differently?

Tightness constricted his chest like a vise. Hot as it was, Jack broke out in a cold sweat. He had to roll down a window and gulp fresh air. God in heaven, suppose she thought he'd forced her to make love? The possibility sickened him. It also scared him to death.

He had lost control. That had never happened to him before, not at any point in his life. Carrying out the secret-admirer ploy was crucial to his and Kary's future. Then why had he gone so far astray and behaved so irrationally?

Jack double-parked and dashed into one of the restaurants he knew Kary favored. Having lunch delivered to her didn't do much to lessen his guilt, but it was a start. He could no more swallow a bite than he could face returning to his house to work.

Instead, he hung a U-turn and headed to Seawall. Red flags flew from lifeguard stations, signaling dangerous currents and warning swimmers not to venture into water over waist deep. Blue flags also whipped in the strong south wind, a sign that Portuguese man-of-war, jellyfish, or other stinging marine life was present. With so many hazards, all but the bravest had abandoned the beach in favor of shopping on the Strand.

Jack chose a deserted jetty, walked all the way to the end, and sat on one of the large rocks. The loss of control was gnawing at him. He needed to resolve the dilemma. And he needed to make damn sure jealousy never got hold of him again. He had made it to thirty-four without suffering the slightest twinge of that troublesome emotion. Why had it possessed him now?

He thought about the problem for a long time, and at last settled on a one-word answer. "Kary." Before her, no woman had ever meant enough to him that she could tap his most deep-seated emotions. Hell, he hadn't realized he was capable of such intense feelings.

He'd approached the idea of marriage and a family from an essentially practical angle. Even the secret admirer had emerged as merely a means to an end. But somewhere along the line, he had gotten tripped up by his own machinations.

He no longer wanted Kary because she was a suitable sort of wife, who just happened to live in Galveston. Nor was intelligence her primary recommendation as a mate. All he knew for certain was that he couldn't exist without her.

He'd fallen hopelessly, irrevocably in love with the woman he intended to marry.

Jack scrambled to his feet. His jeans were wet from sea spray, his tennis shoes squished as he walked back to the Jeep, and he could feel his hair spiking in all directions.

None of that mattered. Nothing mattered, except doing everything in his power to ensure that Kary loved him as much as he loved her.

Karolyn stared at the same page of computer calculations she'd ostensibly been studying for the past hour. None of the data made sense, mainly because she couldn't keep her mind trained on it. She hadn't wasted time going back to the lab that afternoon, knowing it would be futile in terms of productive work.

For at least fifteen minutes following Jack's departure she'd remained in a trancelike state in her chair, trying to assimilate and evaluate what had taken place.

She, Karolyn Lucas, had made wild, reckless love in the office. On the desk, no less. Any of her colleagues, possibly even her boss, could have walked in at any time. She was appalled. It was the most shocking, scandalous spectacle she could possibly imagine.

It was also the most exciting thing she had ever done.

While she wanted to resent and blame Jack for corrupting her, his parting accusation rang in her ears. What *had* she been trying to prove by encouraging him in such shameful debauchery?

The answer came readily, its implication staggering. Unconsciously she had wanted to prove herself as a woman, able to match and satisfy every one of Jack Rowland's appetites. Talk about imbecilic thinking. Talk about misguided. She took the prize.

Karolyn glanced at the half-eaten gyro on her desk. Just as she'd returned from a trip to the ladies' lounge to repair the damage, it had been delivered, along with a note from Jack. He'd written that the sandwich wasn't an apology for disrupting her lunch hour. Still, he didn't want her to grow weak from lack of food. An involuntary smile sprang to her lips. Her life had turned chaotic since Jack's reappearance. It had not been dull. Hadn't she long craved a change?

No matter what anguish she had to suffer down the road, she now knew for certain she would never look back on their time together with regret. Curiously the knowledge bolstered her spirits, enabling her to make headway in the collation of some test results.

When the phone jangled, jarring her concentration, her gaze flew to the wall clock. She was startled to see she'd worked past six. Good, she thought, lifting the receiver. She wasn't overly eager to go home and face what waited for her there.

"You sound preoccupied."

She had let it happen again. Time after time she'd pledged to center her attention on the secret admirer. And in every instance Jack had interfered. *I think of it as reaffirming a prior claim.* The fingers on her free hand formed a fist.

"I was immersed in some interesting correlations between the results of several diverse tests I ran over a long period. They look promising."

"You love your work, don't you?"

"Yes, I do." Once she'd loved it to the exclusion of everything else. Now she'd had a taste of life outside the lab, and found she thrived on the variety.

"But isn't research a slow, painstaking, and solitary job? Don't you ever wish you had more contact with people, operated more in the real world?"

Karolyn sat bolt upright. Pushing the printouts and her notes aside, she propped her elbows on the desk. "As a matter of fact, I've been mulling over that very thing."

A long pause followed. "You're thinking of quitting research?"

"No, not entirely. But I have considered branching out." Pepper was the only person she'd discussed the possible move with, and her friend's position on the subject was clear. Maybe it would be beneficial to consult another source, one more objective. Sometimes it was easier to confide in a stranger than those closest to you.

"What would this branching out entail?"

"There's an assistant professorship coming open at the first of next year, but if I want to apply, I have to make up my mind right away. I'd be teaching molecular biology to medical students."

"Why the hesitation? Are you afraid you're not qualified for the position?"

"Oh, no! That's not my hang-up. Although I've never taught before, I'm confident I have the necessary credentials."

In the background she heard the familiar bell clang of the trolley that made a circuit from the Strand out to Seawall. He was calling from here! She had always assumed he lived elsewhere because of how the packages had been delivered. But there was nothing to prohibit those from being dispatched locally. That bit of information rattled her. "Could it be you're scared of applying and not getting chosen?"

"Uh, I'd be able to handle that, I think."

"Then what's the problem?"

His tone was so mellow and reassuring, Karolyn decided to divulge the real reason for her reluctance. "It's such a silly fear, I've never admitted it to a soul. You'll probably laugh when I tell you."

"You have my promise I will never laugh at anything that causes you distress."

What a kind, intuitive man, one who'd consistently be sympathetic and understanding. A soul mate. She closed her eyes and tried to picture him. She saw a rather pale, thin scholarly type, but what did looks matter when he was so supportive? "I've always been terrified of speaking in front of people."

"Most of us are. They've done surveys and that is always what tops the list of the majority's fears."

"Really?" She had assumed she was the lone coward in a world of Dale Carnegies. "I'm talking real horror here. On the few occasions when it's been mandatory for me to give a speech, it's a toss-up as to whether I'll faint, upchuck, or wet my pants."

He chuckled, but she knew he wasn't really making light of her phobia. "It's well known that many of the world's greatest performers suffer from almost crippling stage fright. But once they assume their roles, talent and skill take over and they execute brilliantly. I'd venture to say the same phenomenon would happen to you in the classroom."

"You think so?" she asked ingenuously. "That I could face a sea of faces and not break out in a cold sweat or otherwise embarrass myself."

"Think of it this way. You know so much more than they do, they will look up to *you*, depend on you to give them wisdom. You'll play Socrates to their Plato." His voice grew more animated with each word. "Oh, yes, I'm certain you can excel at teaching or anything else you choose to do."

Karolyn's self-assurance skyrocketed. That someone she didn't even know could have so much blind faith in her ability expanded her vision and lifted a burden from her shoulders. "Thank you for the vote of confidence. It means a lot to me."

"I want only to make you happy."

"You do," she whispered. A short while later she gently hung up the phone, confronted with a monumental dilemma. She pondered it endlessly until she became aware that she was still sitting in the same position as when the conversation ended, and that darkness was fast approaching. She continued batting it back and forth while pedaling home.

Was it possible to love two men simultaneously, in different ways for different reasons?

That evening Jack behaved as if he'd gone into strategic retreat. He had dinner waiting when she got home and didn't comment about the late hour. Afterward he hauled out one of the numerous books he'd collected on restoration, interrupting his reading every so often to ask her questions. She pretended absorption in a professional journal, but he was plainly more interested in his subject than she.

As bedtime crept nearer, then passed, Karolyn's anxiety level rose. Just when she was on the verge of blurting out her intention of again sleeping alone, Jack rose, stretched, and said, "Think I'll take Rogue out for a jog. He's getting used to the leash and I want to keep him on a regular practice schedule with it."

She nodded, but eyed him warily, suspicious of his underlying motive. He'd had all evening to exercise the dog. His on-again, off-again ardor was keeping her on edge. Just when she was prepared to draw a battle line, he retreated from the field of combat. Still, she should be thankful for the reprieve.

"I'll try to be quiet and not wake you when we come in."

True to his word, he made almost no sound slipping into his room several hours later. He might as well have announced his arrival with trumpet flourishes. Karolyn was wide-awake trying to resolve her quandary with logic. It wasn't working because there was nothing logical about her present situation.

At least she'd freed herself of one bugaboo. First thing in the morning, her name was going into the hat with the rest of the applicants for the professor's job.

Buoyed by her decision, she made it through the next day at work, invigorated in spite of a sleepless night. She was full of optimism, not only about the direction of her career, but also about her future in general. She owed it all to her secret admirer. Soon she hoped to express her appreciation in person. Before he'd said good-bye yesterday, he had made it clear she wouldn't have to wait much longer, that he was stepping up the pace.

Consequently she wasn't as surprised as she might have been to open her locker that afternoon and find a luscious silk satin robe hanging on the hook where she kept a spare lab coat. A lush royal purple, it was patterned with flower splashes in shades of champagne, salmon, and claret.

Heedless of whether anyone might catch her, Karolyn slipped it on, rubbing her cheek against the soft, luxurious fabric. She had never owned anything so beautiful or beguiling.

In the pocket was a note, penned on thick vellum. *I know that your real first name is Rebecca, which means "the captivator." That's what you've done—captivated me. I'm visualizing you waiting for*

*me, wearing this . . . and nothing else. Soon, very
soon.*

She danced a few turns to an imaginary waltz.
Her dream man was so poignantly, poetically
sweet. But there were escalating signs that he
might also be capable of more fervent demonstra-
tions of affection. How miraculous and perfect it
would be if his sweetness and devotion could be
balanced by the same lusty sensuality Jack possessed.

Like a talisman, that enticing prospect sus-
tained her through the next couple of days when
she didn't hear from her secret admirer. But on
Friday night disaster struck.

Jack wanted her. He stormed her defenses.
Overwhelmed her. And heaven help her, she had
no excuse for welcoming his advances other than
the fact that she desired him as obsessively as an
addict in need of a fix.

When her bedside phone rang Saturday
morning and she heard the mystery man speak,
Karolyn covered her face with the sheet. Shame
burned her cheeks; her stomach tossed sicken-
ingly. She felt like an unfaithful wife caught in
flagrante delicto.

All he said was, "The last gift I will send you is
outside your front door. Anything I give you from

now on, I will present in person." She was too numb to speak or to hang up.

"What the hell?" Jack grumbled after the dial tone had whined into the silence for several minutes. He snatched the receiver and lobbed it at the cradle. He'd been a pitcher in high school and his delivery was still accurate. He yanked the sheet down to her waist. "What's going on, Kary?"

Even burning with shame, she couldn't stem her body's unruly stirring at the sight of his bone-melting virility. She scrabbled for a robe to cover herself. "Nothing, uh, nothing for you to worry about."

She bounded out of the room before he could question her further. Taking the stairs two at a time, she flung open the front door. "Oh!"

A large gold Mylar balloon, with COME FLY WITH ME lettered on it in red had been cleverly attached to a sweetgrass basket, giving it the appearance of a hot air balloon. Nestled in the basket were a book of erotic poetry, a bottle of French champagne and two crystal stems, a tin of caviar—the exotic, expensive kind with its requisite mother-of-pearl spoon, and twenty-four-karat-gold-foiled chocolate-mousse truffles, along with other assorted goodies for a gourmet feast.

Attached to the handle with curled ribbon, a tiny note fluttered in the morning breeze. *I will call you later today to arrange a time and place to sample all this, and more.* With tremulous fingers, Karolyn lifted the basket. When she stepped back inside, Jack was waiting. She said a prayer of thanks that he'd had the decency to pull on some shorts, brief though they were.

"What's he come up with now?"

"He says he's ready for us to meet."

His eyes bored into hers with steely resolve. "And what about you? Are you ready for it too?"

She averted her gaze. "I . . . yes. I'm ready." She had assumed that when the time came, Jack would be the one to break things off. This way she could claim that small satisfaction.

Hands on her shoulders, he gave her a slight shake. "Kary, think carefully about what it will mean if you keep a rendezvous with this guy."

"I have already thought about it until I'm exhausted. It's what I want, what I have to do."

"Even if it means the end of what we have going for us?"

She spun away and pulled her robe tighter. This was a discussion she'd rather have avoided. "Jack, let's be realistic about what we have going for us. An affair that was doomed from the moment it began. How can you begrudge me a chance at something better?"

He brought her back around to face the grim

disapproval in his expression. "Have I ever called our relationship an affair? Ever indicated that I thought it was doomed?"

"Not in words, maybe. But it's always been clear to me. When it comes to a suitable wife, I don't fill the bill. Why can't you just admit the truth?"

He cursed when she tried to break free again, but he held on tightly. "I wish you would explain to me how someone with a supposedly superior intellect reaches some of the asinine conclusions you do."

"Insulting me won't solve anything."

"Dammit, it's your thought processes I'm attacking. They suck."

"Now there's an interesting charge to refute. How does one defend thought processes that suck?"

"Watch out. You're going all huffy and condescending on me. You can do better than that."

"Jack, please. Bickering isn't going to help either of us. Can't we be adult about this and remain friends?" She was spouting soap-opera dialogue, but she was a terrible actress. She'd never had much talent for dramatics.

He raked his finger through his already-mussed hair. "Okay, Kary, have it your way. Go ahead and keep your tryst if you must. I won't fight you anymore."

He stormed up the stairs and slammed the bathroom door. Immediately she heard the shower running full blast. She crumpled onto the bottom step, hugging the basket to her breasts. The final victory had been hers.

So why couldn't she stop these blasted tears from flowing?

TEN

Karolyn guided her car slowly and cautiously down the dark, unfamiliar park road. She wasn't sure if it was anticipation or apprehension that had her stomach twisted like a DNA double helix. Probably a combination of both.

What a macabre stroke of fate that after twenty-eight years of steering her life on a predictable course, it had spun wildly out of control in three weeks. For that, she could thank her secret admirer . . . and Jack. Not that she was likely to see the latter.

He had thrown up his hands and charged out of the house after failing to dissuade her from meeting the mystery man at midnight in a remote wooded area. He'd called her brain deficient, then crazy and suidical to take the risk. He was a fine one to give such advice. She'd taken the most dangerous risk of all by getting involved with him.

Initially she had shared Jack's reservations, had even confided them to the stranger on the phone. He'd assured her that Clint knew and would vouch for him. Too bad her brother was on an offshore oil rig and unreachable by phone.

"In the final analysis," he had said, "you should listen to what your heart tells you." Her heart told her she had no choice but to play out the last act and hope it didn't turn out to be a tragedy.

In a succession of bizarre days, this one took top honors.

She peered at the odometer and lifted her foot off the accelerator. He'd given her exact mileage. The last gate ought to be just ahead. The opening appeared in range of her headlights and the barricade had been removed, just as he had promised.

The blood pounding in her ears drowned out the motor as she drove those last two-tenths of a mile and parked in the designated spot. Her mouth felt flannel-lined. Repeatedly she tried to swallow and couldn't. What if her fantasy man was in reality a diabolical, deranged killer who had lured her to this secluded spot to murder her? Perhaps he planned to carve her up as a sacrifice according to some satanic ritual. "Stop it!"

On the verge of hyperventilating, she forced herself to take deep, measured breaths. She was doing the right thing, coming here to meet her destiny. Lord, when had she developed this flair for overdramatization? This would probably turn out to be as transitory as her affair with Jack. Whatever her destiny, it would not be decided here tonight.

Karolyn got out, but left the gift basket in the car. Hedging her bets, she supposed, in case the finale didn't come off as expected. Accompanied by the drumbeat of her heart, she walked the remaining steps.

In the clearing, there was a table with a white cloth. On it were candles, hundreds of them, the flames flickering like a million fireflies, hypnotizing her. And in the shadows, partially obscured by trees, she saw him.

She couldn't make out his face yet, so he might well be the "Beast" she'd described to Pepper. But he most assuredly was not a little gnome of a guy. Dressed all in white, he had broad shoulders, a trim waist, and long legs. A prickle of awareness crawled up her spine. She was besieged by the sudden urge to run, though she wasn't sure in what direction.

"You came."

"Yes," she said softly. "I had to find out."

"I'm glad." He stepped into the glow of candlelight then. "Hello, Kary."

"You!" Blindly she stumbled backward, clawing at the air to maintain her balance. A thousand thoughts raced through her mind, all variations on one theme. Why? "How could you do this to me, Jack Rowland?"

He hurried toward her, bewilderment prompting a frown. "I thought you'd be pleased. I wanted to surprise you."

"You got your wish there," she said, her voice choked with disappointment and anger. "However, I might substitute the term 'humiliate.' That seems a bit more apropos."

"Humiliate?" He shook his head. "Maybe I'm dense, but I don't see how you came up with that."

"It was easy." A wellspring of feminine pride swelled to bolster her. "You really didn't have to go to such excessive lengths, Jack. I probably would have fallen for your line without all the fancy gifts and mysterious routine." She laughed bitterly. "I *did* fall for it."

"I dreamed up the mysterious routine as you call it because I wanted to court you in a special, memorable way, to have you think of me as your Prince Charming, like you did all those years ago. I wanted to be a hero in your eyes, not your brother's obnoxious friend who did nothing but tease you."

Such pretty lies, and how her soul cried out to believe them. "Are you sure it wasn't more a question of amusing yourself while you waited to get on with your real life? I imagine it was expedient to say, 'Here's a place I can eat and sleep for free. Oh, and seeing as how I'm here anyway, I might as well give the nerdy spinster a few thrills.' Well, you did that too." This wasn't a time to pull punches. She meant to rub his face in her outrage.

"You're no nerdy spinster, dammit. What are you, blind? And I never did anything underhanded, either as myself or the secret admirer. I've been totally honest about all of it."

"Totally honest, you say? Then it would appear honesty is relative. I think you deceived me every step of the way."

He held out a hand to touch her arm. She leaped back. "Try to be reasonable, sweetheart."

"Don't use that odious word. And do not . . . touch . . . me. Ever again."

"Kary, I am trying very hard to be patient. But you're overreacting. Can't we discuss this without getting emotional?"

"Not get emotional! You've played hell with

my emotions for weeks, and now I'm supposed to forget them?"

"I didn't mean it that way." Jack flexed his fingers. His chest rose and fell rapidly. "Ah, hell. I can't get through to you. You're distorting everything I say or do."

"Then I'd advise you to not say or do another thing." Karolyn had a reservoir of hurt and anger threatening to overflow, but she was fast running out of steam. Having one's hopes and dreams irrevocably smashed was a traumatic, devitalizing ordeal. To prolong this farce would only humiliate her further.

He looked as if he were lining up ammunition for an argument. She spoke before he had a chance to fire. "Earlier today I told you we could end this maturely and remain friends. I'm afraid that won't be possible now."

Congratulating herself for the dignified, well-controlled exit line, she whirled around to walk away when Jack grabbed her arm and roared, "Just a goddamned minute. Don't turn your back on me until you've heard what I have to say."

Shocked by his vehemence, Karolyn obeyed. She faced him and waited.

"Use those brains you're so famous for, will you? Take at good look at yourself and all we've shared. Ask some hard questions, then maybe you'll understand the *real* reason I've been hanging around, busting my buns to pursue you."

"I don't—"

"Here's a hint to help clarify things. It's the *L* word, Kary, and I wonder if you have a clue as to what that means." He stalked off toward the trees where he'd waited for her. Speaking over his shoulder, he threw down the gauntlet. "Let me know if you arrive at a conclusion that satisfies you."

He evaporated into the woods, a shadowy figure who'd stolen into her life and, ultimately, stolen her heart. Now he had vanished, leaving her with more doubts and uncertainties than ever.

Karolyn stood there in the candlelit silence for a long time, her accusations and Jack's recriminations whirring inside her head like a buzz saw. Her senses were too scattered and her predicament too convoluted to be resolved tonight. At last she extinguished all the candles but one, and used it to light her way back to the car.

She drove home on autopilot and went straight up to Clint's old bedroom. She scoured it for some sign of Jack's presence, but every trace of him had been stripped clean, as though he truly had been a fabrication of her fantasies.

He'd obviously planned in advance never to return here. How *had* he expected their meeting to end? Did the *L* word mean love to him, and if so, why hadn't he come right out and said so? Now there was an interesting puzzle.

She saw Jack as a man who'd always be very straightforward about how he felt and what he wanted. Which led to another question. Why had he changed tactics when he dealt with her?

As she had so many nights when she needed to do some deep thinking, Karolyn raised the walk-out window and wandered onto the upstairs gallery. Three weeks had passed since she and Jack traded small confidences out here in the darkness. Three weeks that had, for her, brought more excitement and tumult and change than a life-time. But she still lacked the answer about where to go from this point. She didn't intend to go back in until the answer came clear.

Several hours must have gone by while she slouched in the comfortable old wicker chair in a self-induced trance. Footsteps on the stairs yanked her back to the present in a hurry. She leaped to her feet, uncertain where to go. "Jack," she whispered, instinctively, hopefully. But common sense told her it could just as easily be a burglar and she was trapped out here with no weapon. She breathed a sigh of relief, knowing she had an escape hatch in the tree.

"It's ninety-two bleeping degrees. Who the

hell left the window open?" a gravelly voice grumbled.

"Clint," she exclaimed, flying through the opening to encounter her brother. He looked beat. "You have nerve showing up at this time of the morning. Especially now."

"Quit your complainin', kid? Doesn't look to me like I interrupted your beauty sleep. What are you doing dressed up for a garden party at four in the morning?"

Karolyn looked down at her swirly voile sun-dress. "I, uh, had an assignation earlier."

He yawned hugely and sprawled his lanky, six-foot-two frame—clothes, shoes, and all—onto the bed. Stretched out on his back, he quirked one brow. "Assignation? What exactly does that mean?"

It didn't take her long to decide to come clean with her brother. He probably knew Jack Rowland as well as anyone alive. Could be, he'd offer her some insight. So she sat in a corner chair and told him everything, omitting the more personal details. "Did you know anything about what he was up to?"

Clint levered up and yanked off his boots. They clunked on the wood floor. Then he lay back down and crossed his ankles. "About a year ago I knew something happened that changed him, but he didn't say much, other than he was tired of being on the go. After that he never wanted to party or have anything to do with women."

Karolyn felt her cheeks pinken and was glad Clint's eyes were closed.

"Started buying all this stuff to go in a house, for God's sake. No fun at all." He was winding down and wouldn't last much longer. "But he didn't tell me he had plans to—" His eyes popped open; he sat up abruptly. "Did that sonovabitch mess with you, kid? He's got to know I'll string him up for making a move on my baby sister."

"Simmer down, Clint," she said, defending the very man she'd denounced only hours before. "Have you forgotten I'm twenty-eight years old? Hardly a baby. Jack did not seduce me." *At least not against my will.*

"Huh." His brow creased in thought. "Say, Kary, let's add this up. He starts collecting a bunch of junk for a house, then he comes back here and actually buys the thing. Next he dreams up this corny romance-novel scheme to put the rush on you. Do you suppose he wants y'all to get married?"

"Married!" Her poor heart couldn't take much more strain. "No. I can't believe that. Not possible."

He shrugged, fell back onto the covers, and closed his eyes again. "Guess you'd be the one to know. Me, I can't think of any other reason a supposedly sane man would make such an ass of himself." He guffawed. "Can't you just see him shopping for a thimble?" The bed shook with the force of his laughter. "And a sweet old calendar with special days."

"Oh, shut up and go to sleep, big brother," she said with a genuine smile. "I can't wait till it happens to you."

She closed the door on Clint, who was still chortling. He was your typical male clod, but he had given her food for thought.

Karolyn didn't need a week to decide what she was going to do. But she took almost that long to plan it. She wanted every detail resolved in her mind. And she wanted an entire weekend to devote to their reunion.

Clint had gone over every day to help Jack work on the house, so she knew he was living there. The kitchen was semifunctional, at least one bathroom worked, and of course there was *the bed*. She waited until late enough on Friday night to be sure she would find him in it.

She parked in the alley and quietly crept to the

backdoor, using the key he'd given her. In a flash she made it to Rogue's playpen, tossing him the treat that would keep him occupied while she hauled in her various props.

His champagne was cold; so was the caviar. She discarded the few clothes she'd worn in her car and slipped on the robe. With a basket in each arm, she stole up the stairs on bare feet. A wedge of light from his open door shone in the hallway. She stepped into the beam of it.

"Hey, stranger. I heard there's a bed in here that needs christening."

Jack made a startled noise and dropped the book he'd been reading. For a long time he only looked at her, but those blue eyes reflected his thoughts accurately enough to fill her with incandescent heat.

"I'm wearing the robe and nothing else."

His tongue touched the corner of his mouth. "And I'm just wearing nothing else. 'Course, you being a scientist and all, I'll probably have to show you evidence."

"Dare you."

"God, woman. It took you long enough." He whipped the sheet aside. She dropped both baskets. In two running steps she reached the bed and threw herself on top of him.

"Oh, Jack, forgive me for being so obtuse.

You were right. Sometimes I'm too damned smart for my own good. I forget to look for the forest because I'm so busy dissecting the trees."

"You're here now. That's all that counts."

"No, I have so much I want to tell you, things I've never told anyone. Remember what you said on the phone that day? That it's important for a man and a woman to be honest if they're going to—" She hesitated, needing an extra dose of courage to continue. But she couldn't back down now. This was what she'd come for. "If they plan to spend the rest of their lives together."

His hands, which had been gliding the satin up and down her back, stilled. His voice was laced with tension when he said, "Say it all, Kary."

She framed his handsome face with both palms and looked deeply into his eyes. "The morning we first made love, I admitted to myself that in one way or another I had always wanted you, wanted something from you."

He nodded. "I understand. Go on."

"What I hadn't gotten around to admitting was that I also love you."

"Kary!" Anything else she planned to say had to wait. He was too intent on smothering her in kisses and she was more than willing to let him.

Long, breathless minutes later she pulled back just enough to say. "Kissing you is wonderful; I may never get my fill. But there is one other loose end I'd like to clear up."

"Can it wait long enough for me to say how much I love you? That I have probably loved you in one way or another for most of my life."

"Oh, Jack." Her eyes clouded with tears, but they were the joyous, wondrous kind that filled her with happiness and hope. "When I was so torn between you and the secret admirer, I was wearing myself out, wondering how I could possibly be in love with two men who were so different."

"You never once suspected it was me? I was sure you'd catch on at some point."

"Oh, I put you on my list of possibilities, then immediately crossed you off. I just could not see you in the role of someone sweet and sensitive enough to court me from afar. In my mind, Jack Rowland jumps in with both feet and both hands swinging."

"A man of action, hmm?" He licked her ear until she was shivering and opening her robe so she could meld her hips against his. "You know I'm always eager to please, but wasn't there something else you wanted to tell me first?"

She stopped moving. "I'll have to keep a watchful eye you. You're much too good at distracting me."

"I don't think I have to remind you that works both ways. I'm pretty enamored with you, too, in case you haven't noticed. So come on, don't keep me in suspense."

Karolyn settled herself at his side and tugged the sheet back up. First things first. "You want the background or just the bottom line."

"With you, I want it all."

She reveled in the contentment of believing that at last. "I was never popular with the opposite sex, you know, like a girlfriend. There was no shortage of boys who wanted help with their homework, but they didn't come around at prom time."

He touched her cheek. "Oh, sweetheart."

"It's okay. I mean it didn't warp me, but it did . . . affect me. I recognized at a very young age that being smart set me apart. The logical extension of that is somewhere along the line I accepted that I would probably never marry or have children. Not because I didn't want to, but because everybody else seemed to *assume* that I didn't. Like I'd have to devote my life to science."

His hand stroked her arm, soothing, comforting. "So when I showed signs of interest, you naturally *assumed* it wasn't for real."

"Very perceptive. I'm glad to find out about

this other side of you. I'm quite taken with my gentle knight."

"Happy to serve you, my lady. Just don't forget the other side of me; the rougher one is real too."

"That's fine with me. I also adore that part." She paused to collect her thoughts, and he didn't break the silence. It was nice to savor quiet times as well as interaction. She would need that. "Anyway, the night of our rendezvous, all my insecurities overwhelmed me. I lashed out because I resented how you'd raised my hopes with the secret admirer."

"You really didn't think I could find you attractive?"

She shook her head. The hair on his chest tickled her nose. She was growing accustomed to the delightful sensation. "You represented everything I never was. Cute and popular. Athletic and talented."

"But I'm nowhere near as smart as you."

"Oh, pooh. Who cares. You're plenty sharp enough and don't try to deny it. Muscleheads do not get engineering degrees from Purdue."

He laughed. "Thank you, I think."

"I'm not saying I'd want to be cute and popular if it also meant having to be a bimbo. But, geez, it's no fun standing on the outside, either."

His fingers ruffled her hair. "You don't feel that way now, do you?"

"Nope. I recently got an injection of social self-confidence. Mom always said I was a late bloomer. I don't believe even she thought it would take this long."

"You think your family will be happy about us?"

"I think they will be delirious. Mom was always a cream puff about you. Your charm knows no age barriers."

All his muscles tensed. "Kary, I have a past. I wish I could wipe the slate clean. That isn't possible. But I swear to you all that's behind me. I can and will be faithful."

"Would you be willing to pledge that in front of God, a minister, and a church full of people?"

She felt and heard his sharp, swift intake of breath. His arms tightened around her. "Are you saying . . . are you asking. . . . ?"

"Heavens, Jack, since you're having such a tough time with the words, I guess it's up to me to say them. This is the bottom line. Will you marry me?"

"Anytime, anyplace. And the sooner the better."

"That wasn't so hard, now was it?"

"Easiest thing I've ever done. I love you, Kary."

"And I love you. I think we'll have a splendid life living and raising children here in our Victorian. Which reminds me, don't we have some celebrating to do?"

"I thought you'd never ask."

Securely entwined in each other's arms, laughing and loving, they gave the magnificent old bed a grand christening. And later, after the champagne and caviar, afraid they might have neglected some minute detail, they christened it again.

"What are you thinking?" Kary asked when coherence had returned.

Though she was joined to him at every point along their bodies, he pulled her closer. "I am thinking, my love, that your standing invitation just got converted to one that's guaranteed to last a lifetime."

THE EDITOR'S CORNER

Let the fires of love's passion keep you warm as summer's days shorten into the frosty nights of autumn. Those falling leaves and chilly mornings are a sure signal that winter's on the way! So make a date to snuggle up under a comforter and read the six romances LOVESWEPT has in store for you. They're sure to heat up your reading hours with their witty and sensuous tales.

Fayrene Preston's scrumptious and clever story, **THE COLORS OF JOY**, LOVESWEPT #642 is a surefire heartwarmer. Seemingly unaware of his surroundings, Caleb McClintock steps off the curb—and is yanked out of the path of an oncoming car by a blue-eyed angel! Even though Joy Williams had been pretending to be her twin sister as part of a daredevil charade, he'd recognized her, known her when almost no one could tell them apart. His wickedly sensual experiments will surely show a lady who's adored variety that one man is all she'll ever need! You won't soon forget this charming story by Fayrene.

Take a trip to the tropics with Linda Wisdom's **SUDDEN IMPULSE**, LOVESWEPT #643. Ben Wyatt had imagined the creator of vivid fabric designs as a passionate wanton who wove her fiery fantasies into the cloth of dreams, but when he flew to Treasure Cove to meet her, he was shocked to encounter Kelly Andrews, a cool businesswoman who'd chosen paradise as an escape! Beguiled by the tawny-eyed designer who'd sworn off driven men wedded to their work, Ben sensed that beneath her silken surface was a fire he must taste. Captivated by her beauty, enthralled by her sensuality, Ben challenged her to seize her chance at love. Linda's steamy tale will melt away the frost of a chilly autumn day.

Theresa Gladden will get you in the Halloween mood with her spooky but oh, so sexy duo, **ANGIE AND THE GHOSTBUSTER**, LOVESWEPT #644. Drawn to an old house by an intriguing letter and a shockingly vivid dream, Dr. Gabriel Richards came in search of a tormented ghost—but instead found a sassy blonde with dreamer's eyes who awakened an old torment of his own. Angie Parker was two-parts angel to one-part vixen, a sexy, skeptical, single mom who suspected a con—but couldn't deny the chemistry between them, or disguise her burning need. Theresa puts her "supernatural" talents to their best use in this delightful tale.

The ever-creative and talented Judy Gill returns with a magnificent, touching tale that I'm sure you'll agree is a **SHEER DELIGHT**, LOVESWEPT #645. Matt Fiedler had been caught looking—and touching—the silky lingerie on display in the sweet-scented boutique, but when he discovered he'd stumbled into Dee Farris's shop, he wanted his hands all over the lady instead! Dee had never forgotten the reckless bad boy who'd awakened her to exquisite passion in college, then shattered her dreams by promising to return for her, but never keeping his word. Dee feared the doubts that had once driven him away couldn't be silenced by desire, that Matt's pride might be stronger than his need to possess her. This one will grab hold of your heartstrings and never let go!

Victoria Leigh's in brilliant form with **TAKE A CHANCE ON LOVE**, LOVESWEPT #646. Biff Fuller could almost taste her skin and smell her exotic fragrance from across the casino floor, but he sensed that the bare-shouldered woman gambling with such abandon might be the most dangerous risk he'd ever taken! Amanda Lawrence never expected to see him again, the man who'd branded her his with only a touch. But when Biff appeared without warning and vowed to fight her dragons, she had to surrender. The emotional tension in Vicki's very special story will leave you breathless!

I'm sure that you must have loved Bonnie Pega's first book with us last summer. I'm happy to say that she's outdoing herself with her second great love story, **WILD THING**, LOVESWEPT #647. Patrick Brady knew he'd had a concussion, but was the woman he saw only a hazy fantasy, or delectable flesh and blood? Robin McKenna wasn't thrilled about caring for the man, even less when she learned her handsome patient was a reporter—but she was helpless to resist his long, lean body and his wicked grin. Seduced by searing embraces and tantalized by unbearable longing, Robin wondered if she dared confess the truth. Trusting Patrick meant surrendering her sorrow, but could he show her she was brave enough to claim his love forever? Bonnie's on her way to becoming one of your LOVESWEPT favorites with **WILD THING**.

Here's to the fresh, cool days—and hot nights—of fall.

With best wishes,

Nita Taublib

Nita Taublib
Associate Publisher

P.S. Don't miss the exciting big women's fiction reads Bantam will have on sale in September: Teresa Medeiros's **A WHISPER OF ROSES,** Rosanne Bittner's **TENDER BETRAYAL,** Lucia Grahame's **THE PAINTED LADY,** and Sara Orwig's **OREGON BROWN.** We'll be giving you a sneak peek at these terrific books in next month's LOVESWEPTS. And immediately following this page look for a preview of the spectacular women's fiction books from Bantam *available now!*

Iris Johansen

nationally bestselling author of
THE TIGER PRINCE
presents

THE MAGNIFICENT ROGUE

*Iris Johansen's spellbinding, sensuous romantic novels have
captivated readers and won awards for a decade now, and
this is her most spectacular story yet. From the glittering
court of Queen Elizabeth to a barren Scottish island, here is
a heartstopping tale of courageous love . . . and unspeak-
able evil.*

*The daring chieftain of a Scottish clan, Robert McDarren
knows no fear, and only the threat to a kinsman's life makes
him bow to Queen Elizabeth's order that he wed Kathryn
Ann Kentrye. He's aware of the dangerous secret in Kate's
past, a secret that could destroy a great empire, but he doesn't
expect the stirring of desire when he first lays eyes on the
fragile beauty. Grateful to escape the tyranny of her guardian, Kate accepts the mesmerizing stranger as her husband.
But even as they discover a passion greater than either has
known, enemies are weaving their poisonous web around
them, and soon Robert and Kate must risk their very lives to
defy the ultimate treachery.*

"I won't hush. You cannot push me away again. I tell
you that—"

Robert covered her lips with his hand. "I know what
you're saying. You're saying I don't have to shelter you
under my wing but I must coo like a peaceful dove when-
ever I'm around you."

"I could not imagine you cooing, but I do not think peace and friendship between us is too much to ask." She blinked rapidly as she moved her head to avoid his hand. "You promised that—"

"I know what I promised and you have no right to ask more from me. You can't expect to beckon me close and then have me keep my distance," he said harshly. "You can't have it both ways, as you would know if you weren't—" He broke off. "And for God's sake don't *weep*."

"I'm not weeping."

"By God, you are."

"I have something in my eye. You're not being sensible."

"I'm being more sensible than you know," he said with exasperation. "Christ, why the devil is this so important to you?"

She wasn't sure except that it had something to do with that wondrous feeling of *rightness* she had experienced last night. She had never known it before and she would not give it up. She tried to put it into words. "I feel as if I've been closed up inside for a long time. Now I want . . . something else. It will do you no harm to be my friend."

"That's not all you want," he said slowly as he studied her desperate expression. "I don't think you know what you want. But I do and I can't give it to you."

"You could try." She drew a deep breath. "Do you think it's easy for me to ask this of you? It fills me with anger and helplessness and I *hate* that feeling."

She wasn't reaching him. She had to say something that would convince him. Suddenly the words came tumbling out, words she had never meant to say, expressing emotions she had never realized she felt. "I thought all I'd need would be a house but now I know there's something more. I have to have people too. I guess I always knew it but the house was easier, safer. Can't you see? I want what you and Gavin and Angus have, and I don't know if I can find it alone. Sebastian told me I couldn't have it but I will. I *will*." Her hands nervously clenched and unclenched at her sides. "I'm all tight inside. I feel scorched . . . like a desert. Sebastian made me this way and I don't know how to stop. I'm not . . . at ease with anyone."

He smiled ironically. "I've noticed a certain lack of trust in me but you seem to have no problem with Gavin."

"I truly like Gavin but he can't change what I am," she answered, then went on eagerly. "It was different with you last night, though. I really *talked* to you. You made me feel . . ." She stopped. She had sacrificed enough of her pride. If this was not enough, she could give no more.

The only emotion she could identify in the multitude of expressions that flickered across his face was frustration. And there was something else, something darker, more intense. He threw up his hands. "All right, I'll try."

Joy flooded through her. "Truly?"

"My God, you're obstinate."

"It's the only way to keep what one has. If I hadn't fought, you'd have walked away."

"I see." She had the uneasy feeling he saw more than her words had portended. But she must accept this subtle intrusion of apprehension if she was to be fully accepted by him.

"Do I have to make a solemn vow?" he asked with a quizzical lift of his brows.

"Yes, please. Truly?" she persisted.

"Truly." Some of the exasperation left his face. "Satisfied?"

"Yes, that's all I want."

"Is it?" He smiled crookedly. "That's not all I want."

The air between them was suddenly thick and hard to breathe, and Kate could feel the heat burn in her cheeks. She swallowed. "I'm sure you'll get over that once you become accustomed to thinking of me differently."

He didn't answer.

"You'll see." She smiled determinedly and quickly changed the subject. "Where is Gavin?"

"In the kitchen fetching food for the trail."

"I'll go find him and tell him you wish to leave at—"

"In a moment." He moved to stand in front of her and lifted the hood of her cape, then framed her face with a gesture that held a possessive intimacy. He looked down at her, holding her gaze. "This is not a wise thing. I don't know how long I can stand this box you've put me in. All I can promise is that I'll give you warning when I decide to break down the walls."

VIRTUE
by
Jane Feather

"GOLD 5 stars." —*Heartland Critiques*

"An instantaneous attention-grabber. A well-crafted romance with a strong, compelling story and utterly delightful characters." —*Romantic Times*

VIRTUE is the newest regency romance from Jane Feather, four-time winner of Romantic Times's *Reviewer's Choice award, and author of the national bestseller* The Eagle and the Dove.

With a highly sensual style reminiscent of Amanda Quick and Karen Robards, Jane Feather works her bestselling romantic magic with this tale of a strong-willed beauty forced to make her living at the gaming tables, and the arrogant nobleman determined to get the better of her— with passion. The stakes are nothing less than her VIRTUE . . .

What the devil was she doing? Marcus Devlin, the most honorable Marquis of Carrington, absently exchanged his empty champagne glass for a full one as a flunkey passed him. He pushed his shoulders off the wall, straightening to his full height, the better to see across the crowded room to the macao table. She was up to something. Every prickling hair on the nape of his neck told him so.

She was standing behind Charlie's chair, her fan moving in slow sweeps across the lower part of her face. She leaned forward to whisper something in Charlie's ear, and the rich swell of her breasts, the deep shadow of the cleft between them, was uninhibitedly revealed in the décolletage of her evening gown. Charlie looked up at her and smiled, the soft, infatuated smile of puppy love. It wasn't surprising this young cousin had fallen head over heels for Miss Judith Davenport, the marquis reflected. There was hardly a man in Brussels who wasn't stirred by her: a creature of opposites, vibrant, ebullient, sharply intelligent—a woman who in some indefinable fashion challenged a man, put him on his mettle one minute, and yet the next was as appealing as a kitten; a man wanted to pick her up and cuddle her, protect her from the storm . . .

Romantic nonsense! The marquis castigated himself severely for sounding like his cousin and half the young soldiers proudly sporting their regimentals in the salons of Brussels as the world waited for Napoleon to make his move. He'd been watching Judith Davenport weaving her spells for several weeks now, convinced she was an artful minx with a very clear agenda of her own. But for the life of him, he couldn't discover what it was.

His eyes rested on the young man sitting opposite Charlie. Sebastian Davenport held the bank. As beautiful as his sister in his own way, he sprawled in his chair, both clothing and posture radiating a studied carelessness. He was laughing across the table, lightly ruffling the cards in his hands. The mood at the table was lighthearted. It was a mood that always accompanied the Davenports. Presumably one reason why they were so popular . . . and then the marquis saw it.

It was the movement of her fan. There was a pattern to the slow sweeping motion. Sometimes the movement speeded, sometimes it paused, once or twice she snapped the fan closed, then almost immediately began a more vigorous wafting of the delicately painted half moon. There was renewed laughter at the table, and with a lazy sweep of his rake, Sebastian Davenport scooped toward him the pile of vowels and rouleaux in the center of the table.

The marquis walked across the room. As he reached the table, Charlie looked up with a rueful grin. "It's not my night, Marcus."

"It rarely is," Carrington said, taking snuff. "Be careful you don't find yourself in debt." Charlie heard the warning in the advice, for all that his cousin's voice was affably casual. A slight flush tinged the young man's cheekbones and he dropped his eyes to his cards again. Marcus was his guardian and tended to be unsympathetic when Charlie's gaming debts outran his quarterly allowance.

"Do you care to play, Lord Carrington?" Judith Davenport's soft voice spoke at the marquis's shoulder and he turned to look at her. She was smiling, her golden brown eyes luminous, framed in the thickest, curliest eyelashes he had ever seen. However, ten years spent avoiding the frequently blatant blandishments of maidens on the lookout for a rich husband had inured him to the cajolery of a pair of fine eyes.

"No. I suspect it wouldn't be my night either, Miss Davenport. *May* I escort you to the supper room? It must grow tedious, watching my cousin losing hand over fist." He offered a small bow and took her elbow without waiting for a response.

Judith stiffened, feeling the pressure of his hand cupping her bare arm. There was a hardness in his eyes that matched the firmness of his grip, and her scalp contracted as unease shivered across her skin. "On the contrary, my lord, I find the play most entertaining." She gave her arm a covert, experimental tug. His fingers gripped warmly and yet more firmly.

"But I insist, Miss Davenport. You will enjoy a glass of negus."

He had very black eyes and they carried a most unpleasant glitter, as insistent as his tone and words, both of which were drawing a degree of puzzled attention. Judith could see no discreet, graceful escape route. She laughed lightly. "You have convinced me, sir. But I prefer burnt champagne to negus."

"Easily arranged." He drew her arm through his and laid his free hand over hers, resting on his black silk sleeve. Judith felt manacled.

They walked through the card room in a silence that was as uncomfortable as it was pregnant. Had he guessed what was going on? Had he seen anything? How could she have given herself away? Or was it something Sebastian had done, said, looked . . . ? The questions and speculations raced through Judith's brain. She was barely acquainted with Marcus Devlin. He was too sophisticated, too hardheaded to be of use to herself and Sebastian, but she had the distinct sense that he would be an opponent to be reckoned with.

The supper room lay beyond the ballroom, but instead of guiding his companion around the waltzing couples and the ranks of seated chaperones against the wall, Marcus turned aside toward the long French windows opening onto a flagged terrace. A breeze stirred the heavy velvet curtains over an open door.

"I was under the impression we were going to have supper." Judith stopped abruptly.

"No, we're going to take a stroll in the night air," her escort informed her with a bland smile. "Do put one foot in front of the other, my dear ma'am, otherwise our progress might become a little uneven." An unmistakable jerk on her arm drew her forward with a stumble, and Judith rapidly adjusted her gait to match the leisured, purposeful stroll of her companion.

"I don't care for the night air," she hissed through her teeth, keeping a smile on her face. "It's very bad for the constitution and frequently results in the ague or rheumatism."

"Only for those in their dotage," he said, lifting thick black eyebrows. "I would have said you were not a day above twenty-two. Unless you're very skilled with powder and paint?"

He'd pinpointed her age exactly and the sense of being dismayingly out of her depth was intensified. "I'm not quite such an accomplished actress, my lord," she said coldly.

"Are you not?" He held the curtain aside for her and she found herself out on the terrace, lit by flambeaux set in sconces at intervals along the low parapet fronting the sweep of green lawn. "I would have sworn you were as accomplished as any on Drury Lane." The statement was accompanied by a penetrating stare.

Judith rallied her forces and responded to the comment as if it were a humorous compliment. "You're too kind, sir. I confess I've long envied the talent of Mrs. Siddons."

"Oh, you underestimate yourself," he said softly. They had reached the parapet and he stopped under the light of a torch. "You are playing some very pretty theatricals, Miss Davenport, you and your brother."

Judith drew herself up to her full height. It wasn't a particularly impressive move when compared with her escort's breadth and stature, but it gave her an illusion of hauteur. "I don't know what you're talking about, my lord. It seems you've obliged me to accompany you in order to insult me with vague innuendoes."

"No, there's nothing vague about my accusations," he said. "However insulting they may be. I am assuming my cousin's card play will improve in your absence."

"What are you implying?" The color ebbed in her cheeks, then flooded back in a hot and revealing wave. Hastily she employed her fan in an effort to conceal her agitation.

The marquis caught her wrist and deftly twisted the fan from her hand. "You're most expert with a fan, madam."

"I beg your pardon?" She tried again for a lofty incomprehension, but with increasing lack of conviction.

"Don't continue this charade, Miss Davenport. It benefits neither of us. You and your brother may fleece as many fools as you can find as far as I'm concerned, but you'll leave my cousin alone."

Beneath a Sapphire Sea
by
Jessica Bryan
Rave reviews for Ms. Bryan's novels:

DAWN ON A JADE SEA

"Sensational! Fantastic! There are not enough super-
latives to describe this romantic fantasy. A keeper!"
—*Rendezvous*

"An extraordinary tale of adventure, mystery
and magic." —*Rave Reviews*

ACROSS A WINE-DARK SEA

"Thoroughly absorbing . . . A good read and a promising new author!" —*Nationally bestselling author Anne
McCaffrey*

*Beneath the shimmering, sunlit surface of the ocean there
lives a race of rare and wondrous men and women. They
have walked upon the land, but their true heritage is as
beings of the sea. Now their people face a grave peril. And
one woman holds the key to their survival. . . .*

*A scholar of sea lore, Meredith came to a Greek island to
follow her academic pursuits. But when she encountered
Galen, a proud, determined warrior of the sea, she was
eternally linked with a world far more elusive and mysteri-
ously seductive than her own. For she alone possessed a scroll
that held the secrets of his people.*

*In the following scene, Meredith has just caught Galen
searching for the mysterious scroll. His reaction catches them
both by surprise . . .*

He drew her closer, and Meredith did not resist. To look
away from his face had become impossible. She felt something in him reach out for her, and something in her

answered. It rose up in her like a tide, compelling beyond reason or thought. She lifted her arms and slowly put them around his broad shoulders. He tensed, as if she had startled him, then his whole body seemed to envelop hers as he pulled her against him and lowered his lips to hers.

His arms were like bands of steel, the thud of his heart deep and powerful as a drum, beating in a wild rhythm that echoed the same frantic cadence of Meredith's. His lips seared over hers. His breath was hot in her mouth, and the hard muscles of his bare upper thighs thrust against her lower belly, the bulge between them only lightly concealed by the thin material of his shorts.

Then, as quickly as their lips had come together, they parted.

Galen stared down into Meredith's face, his arms still locked around her slim, strong back. He was deeply shaken, far more than he cared to admit, even to himself. He had been totally focused on probing the landwoman's mind once and for all. Where had the driving urge to kiss her come from, descending on him with a need so strong it had overridden everything else?

He dropped his arms. "That was a mistake," he said, frowning. "I—"

"You're right." Whatever had taken hold of Meredith vanished like the "pop" of a soap bubble, leaving her feeling as though she had fallen headfirst into a cold sea. "It *was* a mistake," she said quickly. "Mine. Now if you'll just get out of here, we can both forget this unfortunate incident ever happened."

She stepped back from him, and Galen saw the anger in her eyes and, held deep below that anger, the hurt. It stung him. None of this was her fault. Whatever forces she exerted upon him, he was convinced she was completely unaware of them. He was equally certain she had no idea of the scroll's significance. To her it was simply an impressive artifact, a rare find that would no doubt gain her great recognition in this folklore profession of hers.

He could not allow that, of course. But the methods he had expected to succeed with her had not worked. He could try again—the very thought of pulling her back into her arms was a seductive one. It played on his senses with heady anticipation, shocking him at how easily this woman could distract him. He would have to find another less physical means of discovering where the scroll was.

"I did not mean it that way," he began in a gentle tone.

Meredith shook her head, refusing to be mollified. She was as taken aback as he by what had happened, and deeply chagrined as well. The fact that she had enjoyed the kiss—No, that was too calm a way of describing it. Galen's mouth had sent rivers of sensations coursing through her, sensations she had not known existed, and that just made the chagrin worse.

"I don't care what you meant," she said in a voice as stiff as her posture. "I've asked you to leave. I don't want to tell you again."

"Meredith, wait." He stepped forward, stopping just short of touching her. "I'm sorry about . . . Please believe my last wish is to offend you. But it does not change the fact that I still want to work with you. And whether you admit it or not, you need me."

"Need you?" Her tone grew frosty. "I don't see how."

"Then you don't see very much," he snapped. He paused to draw in a deep breath, then continued in a placating tone. "Who else can interpret the language on this sheet of paper for you?"

Meredith eyed him. If he was telling the truth, if he really could make sense out on those characters, then, despite the problems he presented, he was an answer to her prayers, to this obsession that would not let her go. She bent and picked up the fallen piece of paper.

"Prove it." She held it out to him. "What does this say?"

He ignored the paper, staring steadily at her. "We will work together, then?"

She frowned as she returned his stare, trying to probe whatever lay behind his handsome face. "Why is it so important to you that we do? I can see why you might think I need you, but what do you get out of this? What do you want, Galen?"

He took the paper from her. *"The season of destruction will soon be upon us and our city,"* he read deliberately, *"but I may have found a way to save some of us, we who were once among the most powerful in the sea. Near the long and narrow island that is but a stone's throw from Crete, the island split by Mother Ocean into two halves . . ."*

He stopped. "It ends there." His voice was low and fierce, as fierce as his gaze, which seemed to reach out to grip her. "Are you satisfied now? Or do you require still more proof?"

TEMPTING EDEN
by
Maureen Reynolds

author of SMOKE EYES

"Ms. Reynolds blends steamy sensuality with
marvelous lovers. . . . delightful."
—*Romantic Times on SMOKE EYES*

*Eden Victoria Lindsay knew it was foolish to break into the
home of one of New York's most famous—and reclusive—
private investigators. Now she had fifteen minutes to convince him that he shouldn't have her thrown in prison.*

*Shane O'Connor hardly knew what to make of the flaxen-
haired aristocrat who'd scaled the wall of his Long Island
mansion—except that she was in more danger than she
suspected. In his line of work, trusting the wrong woman
could get a man killed, but Shane is about to himself get
taken in by this alluring and unconventional beauty. . . .*

"She scaled the wall, sir," said Simon, Shane's stern
butler.

Eden rolled her eyes. "Yes—yes, I did! And I'd do it
again—a hundred times. How else could I reach the
impossible *inaccessible* Mr. O'Connor?"

He watched her with a quiet intensity but it was Simon
who answered, "If one wishes to speak with Mr. O'Connor, a meeting is usually arranged through the *proper*
channels."

Honestly, Eden thought, the English aristocracy did
not look down their noses half so well as these two!

O'Connor stepped gracefully out of the light and his

gaze, falling upon her, was like the steel of gunmetal. He leaned casually against the wall—his weight on one hip, his hands in his trousers pockets—and he studied her with half-veiled eyes.

"Have you informed the . . . ah . . . *lady*, Simon, what type of reception our unexpected guests might anticipate? Especially," he added in a deceptively soft tone, "those who scale the estate walls, and . . . er . . . shed their clothing?"

Eden stiffened, her face hot with color; he'd made it sound as if it were *commonplace* for women to scale his wall and undress.

Simon replied, "Ah, no, sir. In the melee, that particular formality slipped my mind."

"Do you suppose we should strip her first, or just torture her?"

"*What?*"

"Or would you rather we just arrest you, madame?"

"Sir, with your attitude it is a wonder you have a practice at all!"

"It is a wonder," he drawled coldly, "that you are still alive, madame. You're a damn fool to risk your neck as you did. Men have been shot merely for attempting it, and I'm amazed you weren't killed yourself."

Eden brightened. "Then I am to be commended, am I not? Congratulate me, sir, for accomplishing such a feat!"

Shane stared at her as if she were daft.

"And for my prowess you should be more than willing to give me your time. Please, just listen to my story! I promise I will pay you handsomely for your time!"

As her eyes met his, Eden began to feel hope seep from her. At her impassioned plea there was no softening in his chiseled features, or in his stony gaze. In a final attempt she gave him her most imploring look, and then instantly regretted it, for the light in his eyes suddenly burned brighter. It was as if he knew her game.

"State your business," O'Connor bit out.

"I need you to find my twin brother."

Shane frowned. "You have a twin?"

"Yes I do."

God help the world, he thought.

He leaned to crush out his cheroot, his gaze watching

her with a burning, probing intensity. "*Why* do you need me to find your twin?"

"Because he's missing, of course," she said in a mildly exasperated voice.

Shane brought his thumb and forefinger up to knead the bridge of his nose. "*Why*, do you need me to find him? *Why* do you think he is missing, and not on some drunken spree entertaining the . . . uh . . . 'ladies'?"

"Well, Mr. O'Connor, that's very astute of you— excuse me, do you have a headache, sir?"

"Not yet."

Eden hurried on. "Actually I might agree with you that Philip could be on a drunken spree, but the circumstances surrounding his disappearance don't match that observation."

Shane lifted a brow.

"You see, Philip *does* spend a good deal of time in the brothels, and there are three in particular that he frequents. But the madames of all of them told me they haven't seen him for several days."

Shane gave her a strange look. "You went into a brothel?"

"No. I went into *three*. And Philip wasn't in any of them." She thought she caught the tiniest flicker of amusement in his silver eyes, then quickly dismissed the notion. Unlikely the man had a drop of mirth in him.

"What do you mean by 'the circumstances matching the observation'?"

Eden suddenly realized she had not produced a shred of evidence. "Please turn around and look away from me Mr. O'Connor."

"Like hell."

Though her heart thudded hard, Eden smiled radiantly. "But you must! You have to!"

"I don't *have* to do anything I don't damn well please, madame."

"Please, Mr. O'Connor." Her tearing eyes betrayed her guise of confidence. "I-I brought some evidence I think might help you with the case—that is if you take it. But it's—I had to carry it under my skirt. Please," she begged softly.

Faintly amused, Shane shifted his gaze out toward the bay. Out of the corner of his eye he saw her twirl around, hoist her layers of petticoats to her waist, and fumble with something.

She turned around again, and with a dramatic flair that was completely artless, she opened the chamois bag she had tied to the waistband of her pantalets. She grabbed his hand and plopped a huge, uncut diamond into the center of his palm. Then she took hold of his other hand and plunked down another stone—an extraordinary grass-green emerald as large as the enormous diamond.

"Where," he asked in a hard drawl, "did you get these?"

"That," Eden said, "is what I've come to tell you."

OFFICIAL RULES

To enter the sweepstakes below carefully follow all instructions found elsewhere in this offer.

The **Winners Classic** will award prizes with the following approximate maximum values: 1 Grand Prize: $26,500 (or $25,000 cash alternate); 1 First Prize: $3,000; 5 Second Prizes: $400 each; 35 Third Prizes: $100 each; 1,000 Fourth Prizes: $7.50 each. Total maximum retail value of Winners Classic Sweepstakes is $42,500. Some presentations of this sweepstakes may contain individual entry numbers corresponding to one or more of the aforementioned prize levels. To determine the Winners, individual entry numbers will first be compared with the winning numbers preselected by computer. For winning numbers not returned, prizes will be awarded in random drawings from among all eligible entries received. Prize choices may be offered at various levels. If a winner chooses an automobile prize, all license and registration fees, taxes, destination charges and, other expenses not offered herein are the responsibility of the winner. If a winner chooses a trip, travel must be complete within one year from the time the prize is awarded. Minors must be accompanied by an adult. Travel companion(s) must also sign release of liability. Trips are subject to space and departure availability. Certain black-out dates may apply.

The following applies to the sweepstakes named above:

No purchase necessary. You can also enter the sweepstakes by sending your name and address to: P.O. Box 508, Gibbstown, N.J. 08027. Mail each entry separately. Sweepstakes begins 6/1/93. Entries must be received by 12/30/94. Not responsible for lost, late, damaged, misdirected, illegible or postage due mail. Mechanically reproduced entries are not eligible. All entries become property of the sponsor and will not be returned.

Prize Selection/Validations: Selection of winners will be conducted no later than 5:00 PM on January 28, 1995, by an independent judging organization whose decisions are final. Random drawings will be held at 1211 Avenue of the Americas, New York, N.Y. 10036. Entrants need not be present to win. Odds of winning are determined by total number of entries received. Circulation of this sweepstakes is estimated not to exceed 200 million. All prizes are guaranteed to be awarded and delivered to winners. Winners will be notified by mail and may be required to complete an affidavit of eligibility and release of liability which must be returned within 14 days of date on notification or alternate winners will be selected in a random drawing. Any prize notification letter or any prize returned to a participating sponsor, Bantam Doubleday Dell Publishing Group, Inc., its participating divisions or subsidiaries, or the independent judging organization as undeliverable will be awarded to an alternate winner. Prizes are not transferable. No substitution for prizes except as offered or as may be necessary due to unavailability, in which case a prize of equal or greater value will be awarded. Prizes will be awarded approximately 90 days after the drawing. All taxes are the sole responsibility of the winners. Entry constitutes permission (except where prohibited by law) to use winners' names, hometowns, and likenesses for publicity purposes without further or other compensation. Prizes won by minors will be awarded in the name of parent or legal guardian.

Participation: Sweepstakes open to residents of the United States and Canada, except for the province of Quebec. Sweepstakes sponsored by Bantam Doubleday Dell Publishing Group, Inc., (BDD), 1540 Broadway, New York, NY 10036. Versions of this sweepstakes with different graphics and prize choices will be offered in conjunction with various solicitations or promotions by different subsidiaries and divisions of BDD. Where applicable, winners will have their choice of any prize offered at level won. Employees of BDD, its divisions, subsidiaries, advertising agencies, independent judging organization, and their immediate family members are not eligible.

Canadian residents, in order to win, must first correctly answer a time limited arithmetical skill testing question. Void in Puerto Rico, Quebec and wherever prohibited or restricted by law. Subject to all federal, state, local and provincial laws and regulations. For a list of major prize winners (available after 1/29/95): send a self-addressed, stamped envelope entirely separate from your entry to: Sweepstakes Winners, P.O. Box 517, Gibbstown, NJ 08027. Requests must be received by 12/30/94. DO NOT SEND ANY OTHER CORRESPONDENCE TO THIS P.O. BOX.

SWP 7/93

Don't miss these fabulous Bantam women's fiction titles on sale in September

• A WHISPER OF ROSES
by Teresa Medeiros, author of HEATHER AND VELVE
A tantalizing romance of love and treachery that sweeps fron a medieval castle steeped in splendor to a crumbling Scottisk fortress poised high above the sea. ___29408-3 $5.50/6.50 in Canad

• TENDER BETRAYAL
by Rosanne Bittner, author of OUTLAW HEARTS
The powerful tale of a Northern lawyer who falls in love with a beautiful plantation owner's daughter, yet willingly becomes the instrument of her family's destruction when war comes to the South. ___29808-9 $5.99/6.99 in Canad

• THE PAINTED LADY
by Lucia Grahame
"A unique and rare reading experience." —Romantic Times In the bestselling tradition of Susan Johnson comes a stunningly sensual novel about sexual awakening set in 19th-century France and England. ___29864-X $4.99/5.99 in Canad

• OREGON BROWN
by Sara Orwig, author of NEW ORLEANS
A classic passionate romance about a woman forced to choose between fantasy and reality. ___56088-3 $4.50/5.50 in Canad

Ask for these books at your local bookstore or use this page to order.

❏ Please send me the books I have checked above. I am enclosing $ _____ (add $2.5 to cover postage and handling). Send check or money order, no cash or C. O. D.'s please

Name _____

Address _____

City/ State/ Zip _____

Send order to: Bantam Books, Dept. FN114, 2451 S. Wolf Rd., Des Plaines, IL 60018
Allow four to six weeks for delivery.
Prices and availability subject to change without notice.

FN114 9/